MURDER
AT THE
FRANKFURT
BOOK FAIR

Other works by *Monteilhet* available in English

MURDER AT THE FRANKFURT BOOK FAIR

A Wicked, Witty Novel About the Publishing of an International Bestseller

---

HUBERT MONTEILHET

TRANSLATED FROM THE FRENCH BY

Barbara Bray

Doubleday & Company, Inc.
GARDEN CITY, NEW YORK
1976

Library of Congress Cataloging in Publication Data

Monteilhet, Hubert.
    Murder at the Frankfurt book fair.

    Translation of Mourir à Francfort.
    I. Title.
PZ4.M7755Mw3 [PQ2625.0384] 843'.9'14
            ISBN: 0-385-03453-9
Library of Congress Catalog Card Number 73-22790

To Alex Grall
with respectful
friendship and
profound gratitude.

FOREWORD

The documents that follow throw an unexpected light on what journalists have dubbed "The Frankfurt Fair Murder." The reference is to the Book Fair of 1973.

What is reproduced here was not originally intended for the public eye, and every effort has been made to ensure that it now appears in presentable form.

The facts have been checked down to the last detail; the text has been pruned of any digressions irrelevant to the story itself, as well as of all political, religious, and literary allusions which might give rise to unhealthy passions. Great care has been taken to preserve the reputation of such rare persons and institutions as have any, and even greater to replace with delicate euphemisms any image or expression, any adjective or even hint, that might bring a blush to the cheek of a respectable woman or young person. Sometimes as much as two thirds of a page has had to be rewritten.

A thankless task, but I venture to say the effort is all the more worthy for being invisible.

Further, so as not to weigh down the book with too burdensome a critical apparatus, I have kept the notes not only impersonal but also few, and, as far as possible, brief, though of course it is obvious that they involved a great deal of work.

And so these documents, genuine in themselves, have become genuinely my own, and I should be very touched if, after all this hard but self-effacing labor, the reader sometimes spared me a friendly thought in passing. *Death in Frankfurt* certainly could not have given me more trouble if I'd written the whole thing myself!

About fifteen years ago I set before the public another well-chosen selection of deadly documents, *The Praying Mantises*, which won the Grand Prix de Littérature policière, and, in the United States, the Inner Sanctum Mystery Award. In that case too I felt able to claim a few of the laurels for myself. This caused a friend who is also an excellent critic to remark, "Monteilhet, whose work is often borrowed, is most at ease when what he writes belongs to someone else."

These words have been a great encouragement, and I hope that once again the reader will associate them with me.

PART ONE

PART ONE

From the Diary of
Mademoiselle Cécile Dubois

12/2/72

Our little apartment has been so quiet and peaceful since poor paralyzed Mama gave up the ghost on Halloween. Every day I could issue the same communiqué: Nothing to Report.

Even Gustave never looks at me or talks to me or pays me the slightest attention. Mostly he's asleep, or eating his dinner, or torpid and rapt in thought. But he also spends a lot of time looking out of the window at the traffic down in the rue Saint-Jacques. Then he'll suddenly get excited, and stare, and give a hoarse mew. It's obvious I'm not enough for him!

The monotony of these gray winter days, the lonely solitude of this studio poked away up here under the eaves, and the peopled solitude of my work at the Bibliothèque nationale (National Library), are only really broken on Saturdays, between ten and eleven, by Labattut-Largaud's lectures at the Sorbonne.

Ten years ago Labattut-Largaud was my German teacher at the lycée I attended at the Porte de Passy. And now here he is again at the University, lecturing on Comparative Literature.

At the lycée in Passy, LL—we called him Lulu—was the strangest kind of language teacher imaginable. When the inspector came to observe—for three quarters of an hour every year!—LL had enough sense to carry out official instructions to the letter, and taught us to speak modern German by the so-called "direct" method, which was extremely boring. But the rest of the year he devoted to his real vocation, which was for resurrecting the past. Not the past as people fondly imagine it when they are tired of the present, but the real past, the vanished worlds we continually deny though it is largely they

1

that have made us what we are. LL taught classical German as if it were a dead language. In other words, he turned an obsolete tongue into a really living one, resuscitating not only it but also the whole civilization of which it was a part.

He used to say, "If you just learn German in order to buy sausages, you'll never know Goethe. There are a lot of Germans who know him only at second hand. But if you really come to understand Goethe, you'll be able to buy sausages too!"

It was a tempting theory—that through an outmoded language you could comprehend a dead culture. By the end of the school year we knew a bit about both Goethe and LL—and nothing at all about sausages. But we spent some marvelous moments in the company of two extraordinary men.

In those days—I was sixteen—I had a crush on Lulu for a week. For me he was in the same class as John Wayne.

But now, thanks to Goethe, LL had managed to buy himself some sausages and, after a trial run at the University of Rennes, to win the Sorbonne Cup. He had become one of the great specialists on Goethe, who wasn't a specialist on anything. So it goes.

As for me, I'm under the spell of the Written Word, and I use my day off to improve my mind. It's true I have my fill of books at the Bibliothèque nationale, but it wouldn't do any harm to have another degree. It helps one to get ahead. I'm beginning to realize that a diploma from the École des Chartes would be a feather in my cap. And I haven't even got a cap!

LL himself is still as well turned out as ever, in the old-fashioned style, with the legendary silver-headed cane that only he could get away with. As eloquent as ever, too, with the same gift for making Genius come alive again in the midst of the age it lived in. But the old fire seems to be gone. Has it been extinguished by success?

12/19/72

LL came to the Library this morning. According to Mlle Grivas, he came to consult some dusty old manuscript in the

2

Italian section. He walked straight past without recognizing me. Or I should say I gave a sort of smile when I saw him. He was surprised and reacted, out of politeness, with a mechanical grin. I was foolish enough to be disappointed, and felt I'd made myself rather ridiculous.

I suppose I don't belong to the sort of past that deserves reviving.

12/25/72

A dreary Christmas. Midnight mass not what it used to be. No crèche. When I got home I saw Christmas Day in with Gustave. He's getting to be a problem.

The vet in the rue Cujas says the reason Gustave gets excited and smelly sometimes is that he wants to get married. And he advises me to have him doctored. Easily said!

It's really quite a complicated situation. If I open the window so that Gustave can get married, he'll do the job so thoroughly I'll never see him again, and he'll probably come to a sticky end. And if I keep him in, he pines. But to have him doctored, at his age . . .

He's seven and a half—in the life of a tom, the same age as LL. And as I suspect he hasn't remained entirely innocent, to mutilate him like that would deprive him of already known joys of which the mere possibility is probably a comfort to him. And if he mopes just because he's frustrated, wouldn't he fret even worse if he had no hope left at all?

Could it be that I'm overly scrupulous? Sometimes I think I must be too good-natured. For years I couldn't get married either, because of poor old Mama being so ill. I was just as paralyzed as she was. But I bore it patiently—I didn't yowl! Let lecherous old Gustave follow my example!

1/1/73

I am disgusted. In the crowd in the subway stop at Odéon, an old gentleman who looked as though butter wouldn't melt

3

in his mouth pinched me in a way I can't bring myself to describe. It makes you think about this equality between the sexes everyone's always talking about. What young lady would ever dream of pinching an old gentleman? An ominous start to the New Year.

All things considered, I think perhaps I *will* have Gustave doctored.

1/13/73

I like the way LL, while sincerely trying to understand a certain kind of literary romanticism, is also able to criticize it with an agreeable lightness of touch, even with humor. Maurras, in *The Lovers of Venice*, his book on Musset and George Sand, annihilates them with great competence and ferocity, but his heart is not so deeply engaged as his mind. LL, on the other hand, uses intelligence to order and explain feeling. He's doing an excellent job.

What a pity he doesn't have a bigger audience! At first a couple of hundred students attended out of curiosity, but now there are only about fifty faithful ones left. If it goes on like this, I won't be able to give LL any credit for recognizing me!

1/15/73

According to Who's Who, LL married a Mlle Largaud, and they have two children, François and Chantal. He lives in the rue de la Pompe, in the sixteenth arrondissement. So what? Why should I be so interested?

1/16/73

A surprise. The reference card on "Labattut-Largaud, Dominique" at the Bibliothèque nationale lists, in addition to his thesis and a lot of minor works of a similar nature, an essay called *Resurgences*, published many years ago and now out of print. Sounds rather obscure to me.

1/17/73

Flipped through *Resurgences* in a few spare moments at the Library. Very odd. Extremely well written. But I find it strange, and depressing, that a man not yet thirty should devote his first literary efforts to enumerating disagreeable memories, rattling them off as if he were shelling peas or telling the beads on a rosary.

Noticed one striking phrase in passing: "In 1943, emerging from adolescence, was able to resist the desire to enlist." At last someone who doesn't owe his success to having been in the Resistance!

1/19/73

Curiouser and curiouser! By cross-checking I've discovered that LL also applies himself to literature of the most commercial kind, using various peculiar pseudonyms. There's one card in the name of Battling Cassidy, no less, and another in the name of La Reynière. Well, at least Battling Cassidy won the Grand Prix du Suspense straight off! I couldn't help smiling, but, after all, success isn't easy in any field, and LL must be quite proud of that achievement.

He's certainly a very lucky man—he writes as easily with his left hand as with his right, and hits the jackpot with both! But I find it hard to get used to the idea. This Janus-like activity is so different from the idea I used to have of LL! It's as if his pedestal had suddenly crumbled away. But, on the other hand, it makes him seem more human and likable as a person. More vulnerable . . .

From the Private File of
Labattut-Largaud

Saturday
January 20, 1973

Dinner was rather an uncomfortable meal. It's often like that when Maria-Dolores, stuffed with food and drink and carrying her transistor, abandons us to go and roll in the hay with her Portuguese boy friend. When the maid's there, people mind their p's and q's. The more incapable she is of improvement, the more ashamed you'd be to set her a bad example. But as soon as the cat's away the mice start to play, and the children become impossible, if not downright insolent.

I was in a murderous temper anyway, having lost my nineteenth notebook, the one in which I went to the trouble of noting down day after day the way a younger generation, drunk on cultural revolution, ravaged the heart of Paris and reduced the Sorbonne to a pigsty; the primitive pleasures of riot; and how the bourgeoisie, both upper and lower middle class, got so jittery that for them it was all an indelibly traumatic experience. In short, the historic notebook covering the period from May 1968 to January 1969. Someone had been at my desk again and created a most uncharacteristic disorder.

François, naturally, took the opportunity to poke fun at my old mania for making notes on everything. François thinks Freud's behind it: the theory is that I fill notebooks in order to hold back the murky torrents of time. The reactionary technique of dam-building, in other words—creating an artificial lake and spilling the water over into it so that one can contemplate oneself as in a mirror. And why not?

"Some people can't live without movement," François told me. "But you live in a state of immobility, like a stuffed gundog staring at a bird it can never catch. You'd rather have

6

photographs than films—daguerreotypes, probably! You've already come to a complete standstill at the age of forty-six. You'll end up going backwards!"

Enough to make anyone cross. I was seventeen once myself —but at least I was polite. If I'd talked to my father like that he would have known what answer to give. So I had the good manners to keep my mouth shut. What can one say about change for the sake of change? Except that it's better to stand still and think things over properly. But that's never appealed to anyone except those who are standing still already.

It was foolish of me to ask what his secondhand Freudian interpretation of my novels might be. The novel is a suspect case, better avoided in such a context.

François had his answer all ready. "Your notebooks or your novels—what's the difference? You write notebooks nobody's allowed to read so as to have something solid to cling to. To prove to yourself that you exist. And you cook up potboilers under farfetched pen names to prove the same thing to other people. If you weren't published you'd feel you weren't there at all! Pathological, Dad, I'm afraid!"

Young Chantal gave a silly snigger, and Claire mustered enough motherly and marital restraint to stare at her plate, which was heaped up with the products of the literary effort under discussion.

It's a long time now since my pen inspired any respect in our house. Admittedly *Resurgences*, which came out in 1955 and was a flop, made too many demands on the reader; whereas the other books, which certainly sold better, didn't exactly have lofty aims. If François had only the average Frenchman's critical intelligence he would enjoy most of my books. But he happens to have been born rather bright, so that's that.

He did try to make some amends. "There's nothing to be ashamed of in sweating out potboilers," he said. "I'd place you in the same class with Frédéric Dard and San Antonio!"

Very kind, I'm sure! Only Dard earns thousands with his San Antonios, and I'd hardly double my salary with what I make as Cassidy and La Reynière, even if the income tax didn't filch most of it.

7

I lost my temper, chucked my napkin down on the table, and went and paced up and down in the hallway. And there what should I see but Toby, in his basket, cutting his teeth on Notebook 19!

I feel depressed and disillusioned. For a long time I cherished illusions about the beauty and nobility of education. I believed in it. When I started at the Sorbonne towards the end of 1967, I had some very interesting experiences and felt I was doing useful work. But the crazy, degrading story of 1968 broke some essential spring in me, as in many others. To attain the peak of your academic ambitions while you're still young, and then to be insulted with impunity and ill-used by raving lunatics, and only owe your survival to a hasty few weeks' withdrawal—you can't help being affected by it. I have a feeling culture is in a state of suspended animation. Its last surviving justification—even in the case of my own somewhat unintellectual novels—is that it provides its last surviving hypocritical defenders with something to eat.

But I mustn't exaggerate. My thesis was complimented by a few connoisseurs. But now more than ever real culture is the attribute of a charmed circle. It's hopeless trying to spread it or even trying to make it more accessible. It just doesn't get across any more. The formal lecture, which has come in for so much criticism, has nothing to do with it. How are you supposed to have an active discussion on Schiller or Rilke with students who don't know anything about anything and can't spell, and whose intelligence has never risen beyond comic strips?

Meanwhile I must congratulate Edgar Faure, alias Edgar Sandé, on his latest detective story. There's a highly intelligent chap who doesn't turn up his nose at such a hobby—and unlike me, he makes no secret of it! It's true a man in his position can do as he likes—especially as of course he doesn't need the money!

Would he appreciate my congratulations more if he knew I was a colleague, so to speak?

Anniversary of the death of Louis XVI. He put on five or six pairs of silk stockings that day to stop his feet from getting cold. That was as far as his prudence went.

Was it execution or murder? Such is the eternal ambiguity of history, in which man's preconceived ideas give the same "facts" contradictory meanings. History is the art of eliciting speech from that which is obstinately silent. Historians are partly torturers of "facts," partly dishonest ventriloquists. Literature is more honest—at least it doesn't cheat in the name of science.

At the same age as Louis XVI when he ascended the throne full of good intentions, I was living in a little room in Venice between two stagnant canals, amidst the same delusions that have dogged me ever since. One day I was examining a girl with all the passion of an anatomist, for this was the first opportunity I'd ever had to inspect one in a state of nature, when, as I pored over her more and more intently, she grew impatient and said straight out, "I'm quite healthy, you know."

The enormity of the misunderstanding completely disabled me. Ambiguity at every turn—milkless nurse of impotence, antechamber of death.

But I'm only trying to get out of having to draft that beastly letter. I think it's a good habit to draft business letters. No matter what people say, one's first impulse is usually wrong. And the fact that you're only writing a draft has the salutary effect of releasing your inhibitions.

Dominique Labattut-Largaud   Paris
to Betty Fitz-Delagrange

My dear Ms Fitz-Delagrange:

When Christmas went by without my receiving the check for 1,000 francs that your firm has been in the habit of sending me since 1959, I contacted one of your secretaries on the telephone and was told that the omission, which had caused me considerable surprise and distress, was apparently due not to an oversight but to the cutting down of your P.R. budget.

May I remind you that it was you who insisted on knowing my real identity, after the mysterious Battling Cassidy won the Grand Prix du Suspense with *Sleepless Nights in Brazzaville!* Since then I think I may truly say that I have minutely carried out your kind suggestions and loyally supported the whole range of your company's products. There is no denying the fact that in the eleven spy stories which followed the Grand Prix, from *Fric-Frac in Frisco* through *Empty Tombs in Timbukto* to *Karate in Karachi*, my heroes have been stewed to the gills in either Red or White Zazi, and my heroines, according to their degree of virtue, have quaffed nothing but Merry Widow champagne or Paf-Paf fruit juice.

Not to put too fine a point on it, I find such a modification of our oral contract all the more surprising as the amount in question is a mere token, and our hitherto friendly relations had not prepared me for such a change.

On the other hand, I did receive the usual seasonal parcel, for which many thanks, though the excellent Prince Consort cognac of former days was replaced by bottles of Exciting Tonic Water—which in fact, in the circumstances, I found rather depressing.

Again, my best wishes for a peaceful and prosperous New Year, and hopes that our little misunderstanding will be speedily cleared up.

Sincerely, etc.

Thank goodness that's done! I shall have to change a word here and there, but on the whole the tone is quite low-down enough to suit the recipient and her poisonous international trust.

If the people in the avenue Mac-Mahon imagine I'm going to go on singing the praises of C.F.C. champagne in exchange for a carton of mineral water, they've got another think coming.

I've got more than one string to my bow, too. I can use Aretino's method—blackmail. It would be a good joke to make my characters go green and clutch their stomachs because Merry Widow or Paf-Paf had given them gas! Or I could arrange to go into business with other firms . . .

And while I'm dealing with what François calls my pot-boiling, I may as well straighten out that lousy Grouillot.

Dominique Labattut-Largaud   Paris
to Félix Grouillot

Dear Grouillot:

Thank you for your seasonal greetings. Allow me to send you in return my best wishes for the New Year, both for yourself and for the Grouillot publishing house, with whose growing success I have been associated for so long. Please do not forget to convey my greetings to your highly competent colleagues— Edelberger, our Assistant Director (that feather-brained great stalk of asparagus, Don Quixote to your short fat-arsed Sancho Panza), the charming Mme Fenouille in the foreign rights department (who for once in fifteen years started out of her usual lethargy to sell *Resurgences* in Finland for 433 francs), not forgetting our smart young secretaries—the worker-bees of our little hive (no matter if they do play around a good deal more than their natural counterparts).

* * *

Mustn't forget to leave out those parentheses!

* * *

I take this opportunity to express a more specific wish as well—namely, that the computer which has been leading us such a dance for the past eighteen months may finally be brought under proper control (instead of turning Grouillot's into a sort of Kafkaesque "Bateau Ivre"). I can only suppose it was because of the whims of this monster that the bookshops have recently been unable to get more copies of *Karate in Karachi*, and that sales therefore have shown a comparative falling off.

11

No doubt it is due to a similar error that I have not received the parcel you are in the habit of sending so kindly and punctually every New Year. Your cigars and pâté de foie gras had become tokens of friendship and esteem which I had the human frailty to hold dear. But never mind, that is a mere detail. (An important detail, however, taken in its context. Our business dinners, which used to take the form of godlike feasts at Lasserre's, now take place in any old local bistro. When I come into your office you don't bother to get up any more—just heave your elephantine rear a quarter of an inch off its seat. But, my dear sir, if you don't want me on your list any more, you've only to tear up my contracts! I'd be the last to stop you. The Fleuve Noir people are making eyes at me, and I'd earn much more money with them.)

Anyway, I'm happy to tell you that I am making great progress with *Planet of the Gorillas* and propose to enter the field of science fiction under the name of Phil Anthropus. What do you think?

While we're on the subject, it seems to me urgently necessary for us to make a substantial overall adjustment in our contractual situation. We live under an unhealthy system which combines the worst aspects of both socialism and capitalism, and the continual erosion of the value of money soon makes any contract meaningless. For three years I have been urging this matter on you, but you meet the question with arguments that have not always struck me as relevant (and excuses that don't even make a decent attempt to be convincing).

So I now speak out quite frankly, as friends should be able to do now that everyone talks about "profit sharing," and tell you this situation cannot continue. I begin to feel as if I were the victim of injustice, almost of ingratitude.

I should be very sorry to have to sever my connection with a firm of which I have so many (unpleasant) memories, on the expiration of our main contract, according to which I owe you just two more books. But I hope it will not come to that.

Again, sincere good wishes, etc.

P.S. Giscard's henchmen are asking me for my fourth advance on this year's income tax. They hand out taxes the way Pagnol's César pours out apéritifs. I'd appreciate it, therefore, if you would let me have 3,500 francs. Thanking you in advance . . .

You have to take a firm line with swine like Grouillot.

From the Diary of Mademoiselle Cécile Dubois

1/27/73

No doubt about it. LL has recognized me. Even last Saturday I thought he kept looking in my direction. And this morning, in a pause between two paragraphs, he gave me a brief smile. Very kind and considerate of him, with all he must have on his mind, to remember an old pupil after ten years! Especially since I do my hair differently now!

It's strange how significant the memories of one's adolescence are. They seem more fresh and vivid than the rest. Life begins with color photos, and then they become mere black and white. If not gray.

And that time I had a thing about Jean-Patrick—that keeps coming back to me, too. I still find myself going over and over the purely academic question: Where would I be now if I'd let him have what he wanted?

I'm tempted to give Gustave a new reprieve . . .

From the Private File of
Labattut-Largaud

Sunday
January 28, 1973

At ten o'clock every Saturday morning since November a highly respectable girl has sat in the front row at my lectures on "Goethe and Italy." One can't help appreciating such assiduity. Most students show up only at the end of the academic year, either to make sure they get their duplicated copies of the notes or simply to put in an appearance. The spoken word doesn't mean anything to them any more.

When you come to think of it, eloquence has really known only three good periods: Greco-Latin humanism, the French Revolution, and fascism. In other words, the market place of the city state, the regime of public assemblies, and the sensational early days of radio. Demosthenes, Danton, and Hitler all owed their success to their voices, and all three died because they talked too much. During the Revolution and under fascism eloquence ceased to be an ornament of civilization and became just an aspect of ideological hysteria.

But this girl seems to appreciate eloquence, and her enthusiasm is extremely useful. It's an old lecturer's and actor's trick to select a particularly receptive member of the audience and concentrate on him or her, ignoring the other imbeciles scuffling their feet and munching peanuts. It may be that because of this charming young person my lectures are better than they might otherwise be. I need warmth to bring me out—my own warmth, in the case of my private diary, or other people's, when they don't find me too boring. So thank you, young lady!

I have a feeling I've seen her somewhere before. Perhaps at the Mazarine Library? Or the Bibliothèque nationale?

Be that as it may, I'm stuck for more information about

Kabul. The late lamented Jean Bruce was lucky—he made enough money out of his books to go and check the local color wherever he fancied. What a life!

From the Diary of Mademoiselle Cécile Dubois

There's no doubt about it—LL uses me as a sort of sounding board. It's very amusing, and quite flattering too, really. More and more often he gauges the effect of his words by the expression on my face. When I show great approval, it gives him fresh heart. When I don't show any reaction at all, he's quite put out. But I don't often cause him distress. There's something about him these days that disarms ill will. I did frown at one rather risky allusion, though, and he got the message. Is that all men and tomcats think about?

I wonder if LL remembers that I used to sit in the front row at school too, prompting him now and again with some phrase or name he couldn't quite remember? He used to thank me then with the same discreet smile, just between the two of us.

I don't like to bother him by speaking to him at the end of the lecture. I'm so idiotically shy. And anyway, what would I say? Just utter some compliments that would fall flat and that he's heard a thousand times already? Some platitudes that would make him despise me? What have we in common? We weren't meant to meet, and any encounter could only be brief, a pleasure I could enjoy once and once only. So it's better not to waste it.

I enjoy listening to LL all the more now that I've looked through a few of his Battling Cassidies. They're extremely amusing, and overflowing with imagination and verbal invention. Rather the same sort of thing as San Antonio, but lighter and without the indecency. Like Dard, who's quite a correct writer under his own name but a sort of poor man's Rabelais in the San Antonio books, LL seems to have a strange dual personality. *Resurgences* and *On the Bat in Bangkok*, for example, show two completely different styles and modes of thought. It's fascinating. What sort of a man can he be?

Admittedly the Battling Cassidies don't always soar very high, but at least they do take flight. That's what matters! And all sorts of little details suggest that LL must have traveled widely. He seems to know a great deal about Siam. What a marvelous life!

From the Private File of Labattut-Largaud

From Betty Fitz-Delagrange   February 12, 1973
to Dominique Labattut-Largaud

Dear Mr Labattut-Largaud:

You can be in no doubt about my cordial feelings towards you, and my great admiration for your many talents, but I cannot conceal that the Board of C.F.C. have been very upset by a ridiculous matter which may already have come to your attention. I refer to the fact that in *Karate in Karachi* your hero drinks our apéritif, White Zazi, from the bar of a Rolls-Royce with the license plate 2477 TT 75, whereas in the previous novel, *Kindred Spirits in Kharkov*, he was drinking Red Zazi from the bar of a Bentley with exactly the same license plate. Although this discovery shows the flattering attention with which your books are read, malicious critics have exploited the coincidence at your expense and even more at ours. As an old friend I freely confess to you that your unfortunate lapse has earned me a severe rap on the knuckles.

Mr Borderie himself has reminded me that while it is true that fewer copies of your Battling Cassidies have been printed in recent years, this is because your attempts at diversification, intended to rally a declining public, have reduced the possibilities of practical cooperation between our consortium and the products of your pen. The three historical thrillers you have published under the name of La Reynière are certainly admirable and original, but it is difficult to arrange for Cardinal Richelieu to help himself to a Mayflower whiskey. Regarding your entry into the field of science fiction with *Planet of the Gorillas*, I don't see many market possibilities in the goings-on of apes who live in the future.

But to be serious, what's the problem? At the present time there is a general slump in spy stories, as no doubt in due course there will be a slump in ordinary detective stories and science fiction too. But the crisis can affect only run-of-the-mill writing, and you yourself should certainly escape its effects.

You possess all the qualities necessary for bringing out a really important work at last: you have culture, style, imagination. Everything except perhaps faith in yourself and the power to make others have faith in you. But what can you lose by trying? If you fail, you'll still have the Sorbonne, and that in itself would be enough for most people. You *are* hard to please!

You will realize I am writing this not as a businesswoman but as a friend. I might even say I write simply as a woman, if I could only turn back the clock and make myself as young as you are. For you're a charming fellow, you know, despite your fits of temper and your very difficult disposition. You could charm anyone if you set your mind to it. So go ahead and charm the public, and you can have all the free booze you can swallow. Why not?

Good luck to you!

P.S. I enclose some photocopies of cuttings, including a charming contribution from *France-Soir* which sets the tone for the rest.

KARATE IN KARACHI

Battling Cassidy's fans will not be disappointed. The exploits of his Sicilian secret agent, Osso Bucco Allah-

Milanese, are as interminable as spaghetti. Sometimes the sauce in which they are served is spicy, sometimes insipid. His most outstanding feat is to have some Zazi laid on in the bar of a car bearing the same license plate as that of a completely different vehicle in the previous novel. Can it be that Zazi goes to people's heads? Battling Cassidy must have been mixing Red and White in his gilded retreat in Texas. O Battling, as the poet says, "You wrong us, but you wrong yourself no less."

From Félix Grouillot   February 13, 1973
to Dominique Labattut-Largaud

Dear Sir:

I found your letter awaiting me on my return from New York.

At the beginning of our relationship, under the pseudonym of Battling Cassidy, you had a standard contract with us which applied to any novels you might write. This contract was renewed in 1963 and 1967 by common consent.

In June 1969, at your request, a second type of contract was drawn up, applying to such historical detective stories as were published under the name of "La Reynière." I thought it only fair to grant you this unusual concession in view of the fact that the terms differed considerably from those of your original contract with us.

In April 1972, again at your request, a third type of contract was drawn up, applying to science fiction, which you say you propose to attempt under the pseudonym Phil Anthropus in *Planet of the Gorillas*, which for some time we have been eagerly looking forward to reading.

According to the 1972 contract, you owe us five science-fiction novels.

According to the contract of 1969, you still owe us two historical whodunits.

According to the contract (referred to by you as the

"main" or "original" contract) renewed in 1967, you still owe us two other novels of some kind or another.

But, contrary to what you seem to suppose, even the fulfillment of this last contract does not leave you free to offer any novels written by you to another publisher: Clause 48(a), naturally, forbids you to enter into any sort of competition with this publishing house until you have completely carried out the requirements of ALL contracts signed with us. A publishing house of our standing cannot, as a matter of principle, go sharing its authors with others.

I called your attention to this clause myself. You must have forgotten. On the other hand, while you owe us nine novels, and not two as you state in your letter, according to Clause 49 you can discharge your responsibility with nine Cassidies, nine La Reynières, nine Phil Anthropuses, or nine Labattut-Largauds, always provided the original conditions of the relevant contracts are met.

All this seems to me quite fair and aboveboard. I'd even go so far as to say we've gone out of our way to satisfy your demands and keep you with us as long as possible.

So when you say, "I should be very sorry to have to sever my connection with a firm which I have so many unpleasant memories," I can't help wondering what exactly you mean.

My friend, long experience has taught me that men are more important than contracts. I've threatened to go to court at least once a week for forty years, and only six times have I actually done so, just because certain people got on my nerves and I wanted to teach them a lesson. But I make it a matter of principle never to hang onto an author against his will. Resentment only produces bad work, and it is talent alone we rely on, all of us.

If you'd simply said to me, "Félix, I don't want to work for you any more," I'd have been the last to put any obstacles in your way—especially as your books haven't been paying their way for years.

But you are a special case. I was very impressed with *Resurgences*. It isn't my fault you were bitten by the writing bug and squandered your gifts on work quite unworthy of you. I can easily understand if experience has made you grumpy and irritable, and brought out the misanthropic and suspicious side of your nature. But that you should send me a letter full of commonplace and gratuitous insults—that's quite another matter!

So, calm down and honor your signature just as I am in the habit of honoring mine. We publishers are no worse scoundrels than everyone else. Sometimes not so bad.

Although some passages in *The Pompadour's Cameos* were very facile, others were very good. You know the eighteenth century inside out. Why don't you have a better go at exploiting it?

P.S. Your account with us shows a debit balance of 199.75 francs.

Friday
February 16, 1973

I have a feeling these two sets of correspondence are going to give me a bilious attack. That's the least calamity I can hope for in this sea of troubles.

How could I be so absent-minded? I could hit myself! I could kick myself in the ass with spurs on!

Never mind the tortured prose of that old bag Betty—a mere pinprick on a bed of nails. But the ghastly Grouillot is quite a different kettle of fish!

I didn't remember his ever calling my attention to Clause 48(a). And I still don't remember it. But I've checked, and the clause is there all right, as clear and precise as you please—if you can apply the word "clear" to the Lilliputian lettering adopted by all the grafters whose job it is to take people for a ride. It's the same in insurance policies: the more important the clause, the more invisible it is to the naked eye.

Anyway, why should I have balked? With all his faults, Grouillot is the third or fourth most important publisher around. The idea of being connected with him for a good while was reassuring rather than otherwise. At first glance it seemed a safeguard and an honor.

And now, through his artful maneuvers, I find myself bound hand and foot to a big fat potentate who everyone says is as vindictive as a rhinoceros. They haven't been promoting my books much lately anyway. Now they'll be promoting them backwards. By just chucking a bit of money away Grouillot can savor a long-drawn-out revenge. He brings out more than three hundred books a year. What do mine matter?

What a hateful, humiliating, intolerable situation! The only thing left to do is stop writing . . . or write a best seller! But unfortunately the rules of success aren't as well known as the rules of chess. Yet.

I've got a splitting headache.

Saturday
February 17, 1973

Had a word on the phone with my lawyer, Malavoine, who confirmed that Clause 48(a) is made of concrete. The consultation was gratis because we did our national service together. So I'll have to ask him to lunch. More expense, more chat. And an uneatable meal, because whenever Claire tries to surpass herself the result is a disaster. Anyhow, my stomach's like lead. Troubles always affect me there. It's my nerves.

Had a terrible night too. Nightmares. Dreamed I was being stifled by some huge mass. Several times, apparently, I shouted out, "No, Félix! No!"

Claire was worried and woke me up. A woman's first ambition is to sleep with a man. Her second is to sleep beside him so as to keep an eye on his private life. If you're absent-minded in the daytime you're absent-minded at night too. The next to last time I yelled out "Doll!" or "Dolly!" and it was hard to explain away. The ironical thing is that Claire sometimes thinks

I'm deceiving her, whereas in fact, in twenty-two years of marriage I've only had brief dealings with five or six healthy, hand-picked professionals at the very most. A paltry hour and a half's exercise in a quarter of a century of serious gymnastics—that's high fidelity these days. The French clergy, who've rehabilitated contraception and abortion as the lesser evil, could very well canonize me! Yet Claire suspects me of seducing students. I wouldn't touch them with a barge pole. Since May '68 each one's poxier than the last. What's the world coming to!

But, my taste for men being more than doubtful, the mention of Félix seems to have reassured her somewhat. That's the first time he's ever done me a good turn. And then I was dreaming!

Sunday
February 18, 1973

I'm so worried I can't conceal it any more. I've got too many distractions. I don't listen to what's said to me, and give any old answer.

While we were having dinner I referred vaguely to unforeseen difficulties with Grouillot. They'd thought I was worried about my health, so everyone was relieved.

François told me straight out, "If it's literary it's not serious. Literature's only marginal, an epiphenomenon, or at most a hazy ideological superstructure. We're entering a world of sounds and pictures aimed at overgrown children whose intellectual development got stuck at the age of twelve or thirteen. You ought to get yourself retrained, Dad. You've got a good voice and a certain amount of presence. Why don't you go in for singing, like Jean-Claude Pascal and Serge Reggiani? Under another name, of course!"

Chantal, who takes everything seriously, offered to teach me the guitar. Maria-Dolores could put me on the right lines for flamenco and the castanets . . .

That's what I call a really supportive environment. Alone, alone, all, all alone . . .

Meanwhile, before I go on the music hall circuit, I must go to Canossa and try out on Grouillot some of the charm Betty still gives me credit for. I must go in person. Some kinds of misunderstandings can be straightened out only by direct contact. I've no choice. Since I'm a prisoner, and will remain one for years, I may as well round off the rough edges.

In any case, I can't go on living amid such painful prospects. Yesterday morning I'd have lost the thread of what I was saying altogether if it hadn't been for my young lady.

And my behavior's becoming impossible! Yesterday afternoon Viscount Batz came to see me to ask about Goethe's visit to Strasbourg. He'd brought a copy of *Resurgences* in the hope that I'd sign it. But I took a perverse delight in setting traps for him until I could tell he hadn't read a line of what after all is a fairly slim volume. He saw what I was up to, and is bound to have felt hurt.

And Batz is a man of wit and intelligence, highly cultivated, very well connected. Talk about how to make friends and influence people!

Sometimes I think I don't deserve to have people read my books!

Monday
February 19, 1973

During my seminar on Goethe's correspondence we were invaded by a gang of Danes, who told me they'd come in for the warmth as they couldn't stand the smell in the subway.

By exercising a bit of diplomacy I managed to pass them on to Lavril's Italian class—smaller room, temperature even more clement, welcome more courteous still, if that were possible. Lavril's a liberal, broad-minded, always on the lookout for progress. Only fair he should reap what he's sown.

What an age to live in! Impossible! Humiliations everywhere!

I can't bring myself to go bowing and scraping to Grouillot, who must be waiting like a cat for a mouse—more for the torture than the nourishment.

So I take refuge in memories. That's bad . . .

I think of my Grand Prix du Suspense for 1958 and the irony of the situation. If you don't count *Resurgences*, which was more an essay than a novel, I won a prize with my first book without even trying. But it was just a harmless run-of-the-mill affair, published under a pseudonym. A complete mockery of fame!

And I can't throw off the pseudonyms and come in for a bit of what's due to me at last. *Sleepless Nights in Brazzaville* and similar fancies are not very desirable adjuncts to a university career. The Ministry of Education would turn a blind eye to incitement to murder or arson, to blatant debauchery or diligent production of the lowest kind of pornography. Notorious homosexuality would probably get me promoted. But scribbling thrillers doesn't impress anyone; it's not authentic enough, not sufficiently committed. The commercial aspect spoils the brand image. If by any misfortune I was ever found out, my colleagues would make fun of me, and as for those sadistic students . . . I tremble at the very thought! François is a perfect indicator in the matter—he can make my life not worth living just by looking at me! But he'll keep his mouth shut and so will Chantal: I've told them often enough.

Outside my own family only Betty and the tax inspector know. And of course Grouillot and a few of his staff, but they're bound by professional secrecy. I don't need to worry.

It suddenly occurs to me that if Grouillot wanted to turn nasty . . . But no. What would be the point?

Still, I must go and see him.

Tuesday
February 20, 1973

I've just emerged from a series of hopes raised only to be dashed.

I cooled my heels for an hour and twenty-five minutes outside the padded door of the holy of holies. (Fat lot of use it was being "expected"!) Every now and then Grouillot's shapeless bulk would appear, twinkle across on his little feet and

disappear into an adjoining office, then return to his own, giving me a wink with his piggy eyes every time he went by, and
wiggling his pudgy fingers. He was making me expiate my sins.

At a quarter past twelve I was admitted. This time his
lordship didn't even lift his rump from the chair. I immediately
told him, in extremely hurt tones, that he had misread my admittedly difficult handwriting. A ridiculous scene followed,
with Grouillot throwing himself into the thing and applying a
great magnifying glass to the passage in question.

"You see," I said, "what I put was 'unparalleled,' not 'unpleasant.' Isn't that more likely, after all? Have I got a reputation for being so rude and stupid and clumsy?"

Grouillot finally called as a witness one of his decorative
young secretaries, whose extremely short kilt, secured with a
large safety pin, looked as if it would come undone at any moment. She bent obediently over the letter, opening her great
cow's eyes wide and revealing a pair of lace panties. At last she
said, "It looks to me something like 'parallel memories.'" His
Majesty the Managing Director decided to laugh. He was half
convinced, and seemed rather ashamed of what he'd written
himself.

By twelve-thirty we were in a fashionable bistro for Auverg-
nat chimney sweeps, where my host gorged himself disgustingly
on indigestible cold cuts.

I took advantage of his always having his mouth full to plead
my case, referring to his letter. Since I'd apparently ceased to
"pay my own way," why didn't he release me? Or at least drop
Clause 48(a), which I might not unreasonably regard as op-
pressive?

After clearing his throat with an enormous swig of
Beaujolais, Grouillot observed, "But my dear fellow, if we were
to do away with all the authors who don't pay their way, there
wouldn't be any literature! Publishing is like the races: you lose
money on forty old nags, and the forty-first brings home the
bacon."

I pretended to be a repentant hack in order to get a few oats,
but my somewhat forced humility didn't work. Grouillot has-
tened to load me with crude compliments. "One must never
give up on a horse. Look at Saint John—his Gospel is the best

of the four, and he didn't write it until he was a hundred. What publisher would have backed him when he was twenty?"

He came back to his bizarre idea for an eighteenth-century novel. "Retro's all the rage," he said. "It's a sign of the general feebleness. When people can't build anything solid themselves any more, they go mad about ancient monuments and museums. The nineteen hundreds, the nineteen thirties, the Second Empire—that's what makes money nowadays. In twenty years' time I'll be asking you for a prehistoric novel! So exploit your knowledge and write a book under your own name for once—a bright, ambitious, intelligent book in the style of Voltaire. He's never been bettered. It's a cinch! When it's a question of going back, it's best to be a bit in advance!"

I replied that it was difficult to bring a pastiche to life. But I didn't press the argument. What was the point of throwing cold water on the last hopes the bloated old shyster still had for me?

His mouth crammed full of sausage, he mumbled, "We must get you out of this potboiling—it doesn't even boil the pot for you."

What delicacy! Just the thing to win one over. The swine! He insults you every time he opens his mouth.

Other remarks of the same kind gradually made clear something I'd sensed for months, perhaps years: the real reason for his subconscious sadism towards me. Grouillot, who wasn't even capable of graduating from high school, takes a perverse delight in manipulating people who are really educated. And it's not every day he's lucky enough to be able to practice on a professor from the Sorbonne. What an opportunity for the dunce to get his revenge for all the raps on the knuckles a horde of enlightened teachers dealt him in happier days than these!

As long as I was a good proposition, Grouillot didn't show his hand. But now it all comes out—the old hatred and jealousy the lout feels for the intellectual who shows him up in his mediocrity.

I particularly remember one charming saying of his, no doubt the key to his whole attitude. "I made my way," he said, "with only a grade school education."

So how feeble and foolish I must be not to have succeeded

with three degrees, an M.A., a teaching diploma, a thesis, and a Grand Prix! Damn that Grouillot!

Waiting on the pavement in the wind while his chauffeur brought his carriage, I ventured to bring up the subject of my 3,500 francs. Grouillot whisked out his checkbook with a broad smile—but his pen had run out of ink. By the time I'd offered him mine he'd already sunk back among the cushions of his Daimler-Jaguar, which of course was not going my way. The speed at which that great hulk can move is amazing.

Before turning his back on me he said something like, "Next time we meet, then." There's a delightful prospect!

I suspect he carries two pens about with him—an empty one for the hacks and a full one for the stars. It must represent quite a saving, with interest rates what they are. Anyhow, I'll have to pay a fine for being late with my income tax.

I sometimes wonder whether the time of the fatted calf, after the Grand Prix, didn't encourage me to live beyond my means . . . But I can't be expected to give up our second home.

Be that as it may, there's no question of my going on being Grouillot's galley slave and whipping boy for another ten years. And as—I admit it—giving up writing is psychologically impossible, the only solution, if I'm to hold my head up and extricate myself, is a masterpiece. I'm doomed to write a masterpiece. It's enough to make you jump in the river.

One hope keeps me alive, and that's that one day I'll be able to deflate that pretentious windbag of a Grouillot and see him suddenly fall down on his hands and knees and grovel for a pen. What a ridiculous dream!

Saturday
February 24, 1973

This morning, after my lecture, I gave my young lady a fond look to thank her for the moral support she had once again provided. While I was collecting my notes and memoranda, a student with a beard came up and asked in all seriousness "if it is correct to say that, objectively speaking, Goethe promoted

27

the advent of a classless society." I stood there gaping, trying to think of a polite and intelligent answer to a stupid question. Meanwhile my young lady presented herself and planted a copy of *On the Bat in Bangkok* in front of me to sign.

I was so taken aback I believe I put "Labattut-Largaud."

By the time I came out of my trance the little goose, whose name escapes me, had vanished.

The only time I ever saw her is on Saturdays. But I can't wait a whole week to take her aside and ask her to be discreet, glad though I should be to dispense with such a task. It's urgent. Having that signed copy makes her all the more likely to let the cat out of the bag.

But what on earth is her name? I seem to recall her saying it was something utterly commonplace, like Simone Durand or Dupeigne. But it's years since I've been able to remember people's names.

What else did she say? Something about a job somewhere, and a wish for a happy birthday.

Not much to go on when I need to find her right away!

The whole incident makes me literally ill. May as well try to get some sleep . . .

5 A.M.

It started with the same awful nightmares over and over again—always the same images, as viscous as in Sartre and as gaudy as in a decadent Picasso. I was lecturing on *Faust* in the main lecture room of the Sorbonne. The place was crowded, the Rector and the professors were all there in academic dress, and I was holding forth with extraordinary conviction and warmth. Then, gradually, a murmur arose in the background, and grew into a huge wave that drowned my desperate voice: the Rector and professors and thousands of enthusiastic students were standing up and singing in chorus the overture to *On the Bat in Bangkok*. Then a religious silence fell, and my young lady emerged from the crowd and came up to me, smiling and carrying my collected works for me to sign.

I let out a howl. Claire prodded me awake and insisted on an explanation. Who was Cécile?

Cécile! Bless it, what a sweetly pretty name! It all suddenly came back to me: Cécile Dubois, assistant at the Bibliothèque nationale.

I'll fly there like an arrow shot from a bow first thing in the morning. Frightful traffic at that hour, but I'll borrow François's motor bike. Looking foolish is of no consequence when great issues are at stake.

With a bit of luck I should be able to defuse the bomb.

Sunday
February 25, 1973

I can't get out of my head that it must have been through the index at the Bibliothèque nationale that Cécile made the connection between Battling Cassidy and the distinguished expert on German literature. I never thought of the Library. Neither did Grouillot. Just like him!

What a monstrous place the Bibliothèque nationale is. The whole of French literature, not to mention the rest, snoozing away in that morgue, choking for air in that dust. Everything's centralized there. Whenever a book or a newspaper or a magazine is published, the law requires copies to be deposited in the Nationale. Nobody and nothing escapes, and their OGPU card index gets endlessly bigger. Other libraries are nothing in comparison, as they're all more or less specialized.

I never have liked the place. It's as if I had a presentiment. Despite the fact that in theory it's supposed to be for university graduates only, it's always full of impossible people, especially in the winter—rats from every sort of cultural sewer come to save money on heating. The main reference room on the ground floor is a real thieves' kitchen, with dotards dozing over folios, ancient scarecrows absent-mindedly scratching themselves, and old dodderers running in and out to relieve bladders strained by enlarged prostates. Sometimes there's a waspish argument between a couple of old wrecks fighting the battle of the Marne all over again. Sometimes two dyspeptics grab each other by the hair and make the dandruff fly over the triangular loves of Monsieur Thiers, Caesar's wife, or Hadrian's boy friend. Meanwhile another old fogy has a snack off a treatise on metaphysics. What a setup. And to think my peace of mind depends on it!

But I must try to keep cool.

For one thing, even if my pseudonyms did come out, it wouldn't be fatal. If I'm honest with myself, I'm more afraid for my pride than for my career. But pride's important! Self-love's the only kind that's left when all the others have gone.

Next, and most important, if I can only stymie the wretched Cécile there's not much risk of another one like her. It's just through a series of farfetched coincidences that she's been visited on me.

Another reassuring factor is that she doesn't seem to mean me any harm. True, the average reader finds it hard to understand that for inner as well as financial reasons a person may keep on writing even though he's not terribly proud of what he perpetrates. And yet that's what most pen-pushers do all day long! It's a pitiful, execrable, ruinous way of going on—a shameful disease no one dares face up to.

Yes, my Cécile must be very naïve. With the least bit of know-how I'll have her just where I want her.

From the Diary of
Mademoiselle Cécile Dubois

2/24/73

You can't help wondering whether LL is quite happy at home. I imagine him with a frivolous wife and that boy of seventeen and girl of fifteen—right in the middle of the awkward age. I don't suppose they make a fuss over him very often! When

I wished him many happy returns with that unpretentious little book in my hand, I could see he was more surprised and touched than he should have been by so natural and trivial a gesture. How sensitive he must be! I was quite moved myself —I think I even stammered. How pleasant it is to give so much pleasure so easily.

I had thought of bringing *Resurgences*, but as it was a flop it might have cast a shadow over what was intended to be an agreeable moment. *Sleepless Nights in Brazzaville* was out of print, so *On the Bat in Bangkok* was the best I could do.

At last the ice is broken! I don' feel so lonely now. I've got somone else besides Gustave.

I've been coughing. Must have caught cold in all those drafts at the Library.

2/26/73

What a really delightful surprise! This morning, quite early, there was a ring at the door. I slipped on my dressing gown and went to the door. It was LL, a bit out of breath but smiling, and holding a little bouquet of early roses!

What a shock! I hastily put away a few things that were lying about and made my visitor take a seat in the best armchair.

Having gone to the Library first thing to thank me for my small kindness, and then being anxious about my health, LL had hurried around—"quite simply," as he put it—to see how I was. For some men the most exquisite delicacy *is* quite simple.

And LL carried delicacy to the point of self-sacrifice in conversation. With anyone else in his place, human nature would have reared its ugly head and he'd soon have got around to talking about himself. But LL, with the grace of a classicist who knows, like Pascal, that "the ego is hateful," took an enormous interest in my situation, my career, my work, my studies. Despite the fact that I was often unfortunately interrupted by my cough, there was no end to his kind curiosity. And when I mentioned memories of school, he seemed modestly surprised that I still remembered his lessons so clearly.

Apparently I wasn't just an ordinary pupil to him, either.

And LL is fond of cats—that's always an unmistakable indication of what a person's like. Gustave sensed it at once and was all over him. LL insisted on feeding him a cookie.

Just as he was leaving, LL took a brand-new copy of *On the Bat in Bangkok* out of his pocket and said:

"At the time, I was too touched by your kindness to do more than scribble some illegible commonplace. Our friend Gustave here could write better than I do! You deserved far better!" And smiling graciously, he gave me the new book with one hand, while with the other he appropriated the copy he'd signed before, fortunately displayed conspicuously on the table. Altogether charming.

At the door he clapped his hand to his forehead. "I almost forgot!" he said. "Ever since I won the Grand Prix du Suspense on the first try, my publisher's persecuted me to write Cassidies and La Reynières, and I haven't been able to refuse. It takes hardly any time, anyway . . . But there's no need for everyone to know that Battling Cassidy and La Reynière and Labattut-Largaud are all one and the same. People are so malicious, so easily jealous. It's a fine thing when a man in my position isn't allowed to write nonsense just to amuse himself and others! So we'll just let it be our own little secret, shall we?"

He needn't worry. Whom would I be likely to mention it to?

One other very delightful thing: I just opened the window to watch him come out of the house, and I was astonished to see him get on a common motor bike. That a man in his position, in the middle of winter, should use a motor bike to come as fast as possible to the sickbed of a girl who is nothing to him— what a lesson in simplicity and feeling! It was so wonderful I could scarcely believe my eyes! But it was LL sure enough. Even from the sixth floor I could recognize the felt hat, the velvet coat collar, and the silver-knobbed cane, which made a kind of ridiculous but touching contrast with the bike.

Dear Dominique! How can I ever repay him?

I read the new inscription again: "For Cécile Du Bois, who has listened to me for so long, listened as I speak—from the heart. From her Battling Cassidy."

Du Bois! Why not Du Boïs while he's about it! He lays it on with a trowel to give me pleasure.

Now then, I mustn't get carried away! . . .

From the Private File of Labattut-Largaud

Monday
February 26, 1973

My God, what a terrible morning! First I had to get the motor bike away from François. As bad as getting a bone away from Toby. Then tear to the Bibliothèque nationale at the crack of dawn in an icy wind. But the subway's impossible at that hour, and if you're lucky enough to get a taxi it only crawls.

Be that as it may, I was in the rue de Richelieu by five to nine, and so I had to freeze for five minutes under the entrance to the Library till it was time to rush, with all the other maniacs, to the main reference room, in the wings of which I seem to remember having caught a glimpse of my Cécile some time ago. But no Cécile! For a moment I was taken aback. Had I made a mistake? But a supervisor told me Mlle Dubois was away with a cold, according to her concierge, who had just telephoned. Thank Heaven! But this weasel-faced, slimy, cockeyed personage categorically refused to give me the address. I could explain who I was, show my credentials, beg, pray, wheedle, roar, till I was blue in the face. Nothing doing. He looked me up and down as if I were harboring highly dishonorable intentions. I could have squashed him between a couple of paperweights!

I was just withdrawing and wondering what to do when the typical French hatred of the boss came to my assistance. A girl who's probably a colleague of Mlle Dubois's whispered, "One forty-seven rue Saint-Jacques!" It's also possible that my Legion of Honor pin made her trust me. I ought to sport wider ribbons.

From the rue de la Pompe to the rue de Richelieu is already a tidy step, and from the Bibliothèque nationale to the Latin Quarter is another! I purchased six red roses that cost the earth and continued my martyrdom. Anyone who has never ridden a motor bike in Paris in February with a walking stick and a bunch of flowers has no idea of the difficulties of existence! Crossing over the river near the Louvre, I nearly fell under a bus, and going up the rue Saint-Jacques, I had to endure the gibes of studious youth. It's not a very safe district. The only useful thing the Gaullist régime did was to replace the cobblestones of the Latin Quarter with tar, to stop rioters dead in their tracks. They ought to have added feathers to the tar!

I had to go up six floors without the aid of a lift in a rickety old building smelling of yesterday's cauliflower, and arrived, puffing like a grampus, outside a bilious brown door. An unrecognizable girl with a red nose asked me into an exiguous lair lumbered with petty-bourgeois bric-à-brac and thrust me towards the most comfortable chair, into which I collapsed. I was in the chair where the paralytic mother had given up the ghost on Halloween—the seat of honor. I realized this at once, when I slid backwards on the casters in the direction of a goldfish bowl, in which languished a solitary onanist goldfish. I just caught myself in time, and as I tried to get my breath back I was suffocated by the hellish odor of eucalyptus and tomcat, into which the smell of roses, which my young lady was arranging in front of me, introduced a particularly revolting note of sickening sweetness. It was at that moment that the tom himself, who no doubt, with the well-known cleverness of such creatures, took me for an ectoplasm of the paralytic mother, jumped on my lap, his moth-eaten tail sticking straight up like a cucumber, with the deliberate object of clawing my best striped pants. It took me ten minutes to get rid of the stinking thing by offering up three quarters of a rancid old cookie.

Mlle Dubois is supposed to have been one of my pupils at Passy. As a matter of fact, I do now seem to remember a girl with fair hair who would keep trying to finish my sentences for me and prompting me, wrongly, when I was trying to remember a name. Now she wears glasses, the pony tail has been replaced by a chignon, and the busybody's flat chest is in the process of becoming the enlisted man's idea of a bust. But I mustn't be horrid! Mlle Dubois wouldn't be too bad if she fixed herself up a bit. She seems shy. I'd be willing to bet she's still a virgin.

She's a rather curious mixture of namby-pamby naïveté and shrewd, discerning observation. You get the impression that, in her, the mind has outdistanced the sex.

I got her to talk about the Library, about the six departments into which the factory's divided, and in particular about the cataloguing and card-index systems in the section for which she's partly responsible—the section that deals with issuing modern works to be read on the spot.

It was clearly not difficult for a practiced librarian, once her interest was awakened, to make me that unexpected birthday present. The École des Chartes gives it students more than just another degree, another bit of parchment—it imparts a state of mind, a vocation. A "chartist" is congenitally nosy, with a sixth sense for comparing and deciphering texts and wringing confessions out of the merest comma. And girls are naturally inquisitive. So put a female "chartist" among six million books and there's the devil to pay!

But as I had thought, there are not likely to be two devils there to bother about me. If Cécile hadn't been coming to my Saturday lectures, she'd never have thought of hunting me from card to card through the index as if she were chasing a rabbit from hole to hole.

And, as I'd also thought, her intentions are of the best. You might even say she's overflowing with good will. At the worst, she might have wanted to pay me what she thought was a flattering attention in order to do herself a bit of good in the exam. There's a one-in-three chance of her getting me in the oral, and she must have a good idea that I'm in a position to pass her.

And she was certainly marvelous at seizing the opportunity to be courteously discreet.

Everything's in order. I can rest easy, as far as that's possible. But what a close shave! My knees are still weak!

When I think of the peace and quiet I'd be enjoying if I

hadn't flung myself blindly into writing! But, good or bad, I've acquired a place in the republic of letters, and, like a prisoner looking at the sky through the bars, I can't stifle the stubborn, irresistible hope of success. What would I do on a desert island? I'd write on the sand when the tide was out to entertain the fish when it was in.

Saturday
March 3, 1973

I thought all those upsets and emotions were going to give me a bilious attack, and now I too have caught a cold, from my adventure on the heights of the rue Saint-Jacques. I've stayed in my room since Wednesday, enjoying a well-earned irresponsibility after so many agitations and tempests in a teacup. I'm feeling better now, thank God!

When she saw I wasn't in the Saint-Just lecture room this morning, Cécile telephoned to ask how I was, then came around at about four and dug herself in till seven. It was a restful conversation. The main subject was Gustave, whom his chaste mistress hesitates to have doctored. To pass the time, I went into the question thoroughly from every point of view—anatomical, physiological, psychological, Freudian, moral, social, global, structural—and came to the conclusion that it was metaphysically impossible to decide. If God does not allow us to be reborn in the company of our pets, Gustave can certainly be cut to pieces with impunity. But if we are fortunate enough to come to life again with our cats, then the question is whether doctored toms revive as eunuchs or intact. To cause Gustave to be doctored forever would obviously be a very weighty responsibility. Cécile was much impressed.

She's a bit of a clinger, but not dangerous. And this evening, hanging on my lips, drinking in every word, she was almost pretty. The setting suited her—she seemed to like the period furniture.

Claire was jealous and made excuses to hang around. I so rarely entertain any woman but her in our room! When Cécile had gone, I told her about the *On the Bat* incident, and she had a good laugh. It's easy to laugh—afterwards.

I ought to confide in Claire more often. It would be a relief. But each of us lives for himself, sleeps for himself, makes love for himself.

I've had the time to ponder Grouillot's eighteenth-century suggestion. Not feasible.

I've noticed an alarming thing. When everything was going well and I was as happy as possible, I used to like to read certain passages in my notebooks. But now that everything has gone wrong, and the spirit of the Sorbonne has been murdered, and the children slip between my fingers like smoke, and Claire herself takes refuge in everyday tasks, I've given that habit up —it had started to hurt. And yet I go on pouring it all out alone in my well-heated study. It's absurd. The public has gone off me just as I've gone off my own notebooks, and I go on writing, just as incontinent as Gustave! But who's going to doctor me?

Sunday
March 4, 1973

Claire shook me awake at daybreak. I was moaning in a hollow voice, "My children! My poor children . . ."

If I'm woken up in the middle of a nightmare, it often keeps pursuing me after I'm awake. And this time it was the worst nightmare I've ever had or ever shall.

I was in an eighteenth-century cottage, putting the finishing touches to a long novel. All around the rickety table a string of starving infants—François, Chantal, and all those I lacked the conviction to have—watched me in silence, with heart-rending hope. Also gazing at me, from a corner, was our one and only cow. Its milk had turned, and in its big wet eyes I could read a poignant appeal. (Claire wasn't in the dream. Freud would say she was the cow.) For the first time, I had managed to produce a distinguished novel—a masterly combination of Marivaux, Prévost, and Choderlos de Laclos.

37

Then I suddenly saw that the pile of pages had disappeared! Little Chantal led me by the hand to a childish, flowery drawing stuck up on the wall. In capital letters, the words: HAPPY BIRTHDAY, DADDY. I turned the drawing over and read:

"FOREWORD

"It is not without misgivings that a man of quality . . ."

I let out a howl of pain and fear. Where had the other pages got to? François explained that he'd sold them to the neighboring shopkeepers, who were always short of paper.

I rushed out of the house, with the snow thick on the ground, and ran to the village to rescue at least some of the best pages, so that they would remain for posterity like fragments of Aristotle or Lucretius. My masterpiece being used to wrap hunks of meat, slices of pâté, or pints of chestnuts (N.B. all "potboiling" products!), and I hadn't got a penny to buy back a single wrapping. In the end I flung myself on the conclusion of my book and ran off ignominiously with the dogs at my heels, clutching to my bosom a parcel that palpitated there like another heart in distress—a pound of calves' lungs for the cat.

Then there was a break in the continuity, and I could see myself now, rowing in a galley over a raging sea among a lot of Protestants who never stopped protesting. It must have been then I groaned.

One strange thing that shows the high degree of elaboration reached in certain dreams is a phrase I can recall very exactly: "I'm going to throw myself in the water, and then I shan't hear any more about myself."

That was where I really touched bottom. And it's no doubt correct to see it as a kind of warning. My poor novels! My poor children! Everything I've produced seems doomed to sterility. A psychiatrist would probably say condescendingly that I had a "failure complex." But is it my fault if society is what it is, both for writers and for children?

One thing's certain: I can no longer give François and Chantal anything but a purely negative education.

In the classical period, where admittedly children weren't accorded enough importance, at least people revered the old and respected men of achievement. But the fascist, Marxist, and democratic myths have made young people insolent, and all the more aggressive because they really feel more threatened, enjoying a state of privilege which is unsound and only temporary. On the one hand they grow old quickly, and on the other they have difficulty being born. The adolescent of today knows very well he's only escaped fetal massacre by chance in order to become an unwanted old man, himself doomed to euthanasia. The prospect is enough to upset anyone's equilibrium.

One doesn't have to be a pessimist to feel helpless and disturbed at such a state of affairs. I feel so powerless I don't even react any more to François's taunts or Chantal's casualness, which their mother always backs up if only by silence. "How can you, who do so much talking and writing," she says, "still take words seriously?"

Yes, I know. Having misused words, the world of today is now suffering from their devaluation. Anyone can say or write anything with impunity. The public is blasé and skeptical, and wallows in more concrete kinds of satisfaction.

Just the same, the world began with words: "Let there be light!" But where's our light got to now? What have we done with it?

Despite all my faults I still love words and take pride in their importance—the importance they no longer have but which they must recover. If only I could one day write a book which had the verbal density of creation! O Lord, hear my prayer!

Monday
March 5, 1973

TEN OR TWELVE!!! In the middle of the night I had a sudden revelation. In a second everything fell into place. In a flash I'd surveyed, seen, foreseen all! What a marvelous recollection. Heavenly music. TEN OR TWELVE!!! TEN OR TWELVE!!!

Now the white light of dawn is creeping into my study. The fever has passed. It's time to see things clearly and think them over carefully.

Last night when I was trying to get to sleep and Claire had turned her back on me, I happened by the merest chance to open the Encyclopedia universalis at page 549 of the thirteenth volume—the article on Prévost. I fell asleep after I'd read the introduction in large print, which deserves to be quoted in full:

"Prévost d'Exiles is a man of contradictions: now monk, now soldier, now Jansenist, now Jesuit, now Christian moralist, and now libertine philosopher, he belonged to no sect or party. He did not feel free either in France or England or Holland; He dreamed of escape but always returned to his chains; Nowhere was home for him—as he declared in the name he adopted, he was a man 'of exiles.' But he ruled as king over his griefs and dreams, and wrote ten or twelve novels, some of them interminable, many of them unfinished, composed one after another yet connected and forming a single human comedy, uncertain and poignant. But one brief tale more enigmatic and ambiguous than the others has eclipsed all the rest; *Manon Lescaut* helps to hide from us the real Prévost and one of the great novelistic achievements of the eighteenth century. True, the book itself is contradictory, improvised, random; but as a voyage through the 'subterranean universe' of the heart, written at a time when irony, wit, and savoir-faire often stood in for genius, this dangerous journey remains an unparalleled adventure."

Ten or twelve novels! When I first read the words the vagueness didn't strike me. But when the fatal figures rang in my ears in sleep and good old Abbé Antoine François Prévost mischievously came and said at my bedside, "I wrote the eleventh for you!" then how could I not be overwhelmed and full of hope?

And it's not only Jean Sgard of the University of Grenoble who can't get closer than two to the number of novels Prévost turned out.* The eminent Louis Bovey, in his learned intro-

* Editor's note: Monsieur Jean Sgard was kind enough to explain the mystery in a letter dated September 5, 1974, in which he writes as follows: "Prévost wrote ten novels in the strict sense of the word; to these might be added *Les Aventures de Pomponius* (*The Adventures of Pomponius*), of which he completed half, and a large collection of tales and short stories published in his periodical, *Le Pour et Contre* (*For and Against*); that makes a total of twelve." The reader will observe, both in the introduction to the article referred to in the text and in the passage just quoted that Monsieur Sgard uses the semicolon in a natural and

duction to the umpteenth edition of *Manon Lescaut*, published in 1961 by the "Cercle du Bibliophile" (Booklovers' Club) in Paris, says calmly—I've just checked: "No one nowadays dreams of taking down from the shelves of oblivion any of the other twenty novels published by Prévost out of an impressive total of more than a hundred and ten volumes."

According to the undisputed expert, Jean Sgard, and to Louis Bovey, the Abbé produced either ten or twelve or twenty-one novels, and as for the number of volumes—there are so many his own mother wouldn't know them! Marvelous! And so encouraging!

Prévost is in fact an almost unique case in the history of literature—an extremely prolific and often distinguished writer who produced "more than a hundred and ten volumes" which all fell into oblivion for nearly two hundred years, with the exception of the *Histoire du chevalier des Grieux et de Manon Lescaut*, which has been an enormous and universal success since 1731. There are new editions all the time in every language; operas; films. Both for the general public and for the more literary, Prévost is Manon. And most academic as well as fashionable critics have always flung themselves on poor Manon like so many syphilis treponemae and neglected all the rest. Incredible but true!

What happened to the first six volumes of the *Mémoires et Aventures d'un homme de qualité*, of which the engaging *Manon* is only the seventh? And the eight volumes of *Cleveland*? And the six of *Le Doyen de Killerine*? And *Les Mémoires d'un honnête homme*? And *Le Monde moral*? Not to mention the fifteen volumes of the *Histoire des voyages*, or the books on history.

It's quite simple. Between 1810 and 1816 a trifling matter of thirty-nine volumes of selections from Prévost were published in Paris. (Apart from *Manon*, he was already being published in selections by the end of the eighteenth century!) After that, as far as I know and with the exception of *Manon*, nothing from that day to this.

---

just manner, denoting a writer of the first order. I did not enter into correspondence with Louis Bovey, not wishing to bother him if he was still alive.

Oh, but I was forgetting the *Histoire d'une Grecque moderne*, which the "10/18" series worthily issued recently in paperback, with an excellent introduction. But this fascinating volume hasn't been as widely read as it deserves.

In short, but for two volumes, "one of the great novelistic achievements of the eighteenth century" is buried in a few public and private libraries, and no one much cares.

Suppose I were to plagiarize a Prévost? Who'd notice?

A Prévost! What a windfall for an unfortunate author who has to produce a masterpiece! The lazy mob of critics has maintained from generation to generation that only *Manon* is any good—if only to get out of having to read the rest!—but the resurrection of *L'Histoire d'une Grecque* has just proved the opposite, and the devil must be in it if, by dint of looking carefully . . .

But best not mention the devil in connection with a windfall from Prévost. There's a well-known story that when he was appointed chaplain to the Prince de Conti, the Prince said, "I must warn you, my dear Abbé, that I never go to mass," and Prévost answered, "Excellent, Your Highness—I never celebrate it!" And if my memory serves, he was converted to Protestantism in 1728 in order to obtain a passport and returned to the Catholic fold in 1734 in order to obtain a residence permit. Perhaps this windfall from one of the pioneers of ecumenism has a whiff of brimstone about it? Perhaps it's really a pitfall?

There it goes! The transistor! Maria-Dolores is back! Every time she comes away from her Portuguese's flea-bitten room she performs a fanfare on that yowler! Not only, in obedience to the unions, do I have to feed the shameless hussy filet mignon when we have steak tartare, but I have to put up with this hullabaloo as well.

The present number is a visceral anarchist chant by Joan Baez. In her private diary, which she leaves lying all over the place, Chantal innocently but indecently renders the name as "John Baise." How sweet!

I shan't write any more today.

I keep going through alternate phases of hope and discouragement. I get intoxicated, and then I sober up again. To plagiarize a Prévost! What an enormous stunt. A bit too much of one, perhaps!

But there are favorable circumstances and disturbing coincidences which are very seductive. Sometimes they seem almost miraculous—or like a sort of predestination.

When I read *Manon* and *L'Histoire d'une Grecque moderne* I already felt a kind of secret affinity between Prévost and myself, and Sgard's excellent article put the finishing touch. I quote some of his most penetrating remarks:

"His attempts to rehabilitate his own life led him towards a narrative method that was radically new. He wrote his novels in the form of pseudohistorical memoirs; they are private lives told in the first person singular in an attempt at justification; but the argument is always the same: that appearances are false, and that the only thing which counts is the truth of the heart. Every Prévost novel is an emotional apologia, a protest against the concatenations of fate . . ." (Here I replace a semicolon with dots.) "Prévost is perfectly well aware of the danger inherent in this rhetoric of sincerity, but he considers it inevitable. He is convinced that every human being is the prisoner of his own vision, imagination, and passions, and he, Prévost, merely tries to give an account of the fundamental intentions of each of his narrators, when necessary allowing them to become entangled in their own errors, blindness, and folly. Each one is both guilty and touching, each is a living problem and the accused in a trial which can never arrive at a verdict. So truth belongs to no one, and Prévost has made sure that it escapes us too . . . Testimonies are juxtaposed and contradict each other . . . Prévost, painter of subjectivity, insincerity, the heart's contradictions, journeys through a sort of 'subterranean universe,' the realm of the irrational. His work presents dream, anguish, emotional intoxication, the cruelty of love . . . But nothing could be more deliberate than this descent into the realm of the shades . . ."

How modern it all sounds, and how relevant to me!

Prévost lived at a watershed in history, when the disenchanted reason of the eighteenth century was already struggling with the sensibility of approaching romanticism—which still goes on making converts under one name or another. And while he sought to establish a balance, Prévost adapted his forms of expression to the dichotomy. I also, a little too intelligent and a lot too sensitive, sought in *Resurgences* and continue to seek in my notebooks an equilibrium which always eludes me.

Sgard's last observation is particularly brilliant: "He is a writer of the Enlightenment, certainly, but a religious writer for whom enlightenment would be nothing if it did not illumine Evil." What skill in the use of captials! The fellow can definitely write better than he can count.†

Yes, if Prévost does give me a helping hand, the thing will go off all the better for our having preoccupations in common and the same method of giving them expression.

But there is one particular circumstance which weighs considerably in the argument: Prévost retained the classical form, and setting plays no part in his work. Man is what interests him, not his trousers. And as human nature hasn't changed at all in two hundred years, a psychological novel of the eighteenth century is still perfectly valid for the reader of today. I shouldn't have to make many changes in what I borrow: it would seem as modern as well, as *L'Histoire d'une Grecque moderne!* That should please that philistine of a Grouillot—just what he wants.

How tempting!

Mlle Dubois phoned at one o'clock to ask how I was. I reassured her. The phone makes her voice sound intelligent and resonant. I shall have to take the young lady out one of these days to make sure she stays well disposed.

† Editor's note: See note, pp. 40–41.

From the Diary of
Mademoiselle Cécile Dubois

3/7/73

I've been more dead than alive for the past three days. Gustave ran away on Monday morning at eight o'clock, first through the hallway and then through the air vent, left open by the concierge despite my requests to the contrary. I thought I'd never see him again. And I worried all the time at the Library, imagining him mewing at the door or the window, a little repentant mew, and me not there to let him in. But at last, at last, he came back at six o'clock this evening. I suppose he didn't fancy a third night out of doors in this weather. But, heavens, the state he was in! His ears all torn and his tail full of soot. Unrecognizable! I had to give him a bath in the washbasin, a thing he loathes. But it was him, all right—I could tell by the voice!

For two nights I'd been awakened by the awful yowls of tomcats fighting. I kept asking myself, "Is that my Gustave?" It wasn't easy, among those hysterical snarls, to identify the measured tones of a familiar companion. How love changes people!

Yesterday, on the phone, I didn't like to mention my worry to Dominique. He would have laughed at me . . . and so would the concierge, who was listening in though she pretended not to. Already last Saturday, when I asked LL whether he thought an operation was advisable, he didn't take the matter very seriously. And yet, despite certain fleeting appearances to the contrary, Dominique is not unfeeling. He's egocentric, hiding an excess of sensibility beneath an easy irony. And I must say in his defense that my affection for the cat could well seem to him excessive and slightly absurd. He doesn't realize how few contacts I have, by the very nature of things. He

45

doesn't know that Gustave, with both his fidelity and his faults, is all that's left me of poor Mama. I can see him now, rubbing himself against her as she sat there motionless. It was almost indecent. But as far as emotion's concerned, people have such memories as they can.

Dominique made some vague mention of asking me out, which was very nice of him.

When I went to see him in his handsome Directoire-Return-from-Egypt flat, he let fall a remark about women in trousers which made me feel those I was wearing were out of place. But pants are very practical in winter, and you feel safer in the subway. I shall go to the Bon Marché and buy a little gray jersey dress.

LL's wife—tall and thin and very bourgeois—is not very agreeable. But that's of no importance. All that matters is that Dominique's better.

From the Private File of Labattut-Largaud

Wednesday
March 7, 1973

I'm up in the clouds and even talk to myself, as always when I am obsessed by a subject. I imagine things that are really positively delicious . . .

That Malthusian of a Grouillot would print about four or five thousand copies of my eighteenth-century effort. I'd wait for them all to be sent out, for a little stir of curiosity to make people buy up about a quarter of them, and for the rancorous critics to dole out a few noncommittal compliments, and then I'd go and see Grouillot bearing a photocopy version of the original racy volume, unpublished since the First Empire. What a delightful scene!

"So, my dear Grouillot, you're bringing out a new edition of Prévost? . . . Prévost! Surely you've heard of him? Antoine François! An Abbé, died at Courteuil, between Senlis and Chantilly, on September 25, 1763. . . . *Manon*—right, you've got it! Little Manon. There's only one. There's an opera by Massenet and a film by Henri-Georges Clouzot . . . Didn't you recognize the style? And didn't your reading committee recognize it either? I admit my styles *are* very varied, what with *Resurgences* and *Sleepless Nights in Brazzaville!*

"Come now, pull yourself together. Have swig of Beaujolais to help wash the sausages down. It's not so bad as all that. All you have to do is withdraw the book and say there's some production fault. That's nothing for a publisher . . .

"You don't intend to sue me? I think you're quite right. You wouldn't come out of it very well. What's the point in advertising your extraordinary ignorance, your crass lack of culture, your sublime incompetence? Why create for me at your own expense the flattering reputation of being an intellectual practical joker, a learned troubadour letting off steam? . . .

"You say I should keep quiet? What, when everyone would be so amused and the joke would give Gallimard and Hachette such pleasure? It's not every day those two are both pleased at the same time! But I will keep it to myself just the same, because you're my friend.

"You don't look quite so pale now. By the way, here's an offer I've had from the 'Fleuve Noir' people. Interesting, isn't it? *They*'re very well organized! . . .

"You suggest I still keep up a connection with you too? But of course! After all the memories we share, all your kindnesses . . . Yes, thanks, I don't mind if I do have a havana. Waiter! A bottle of Veuve-Clicquot brut!

"Let's say no more about Clause 48(a)! It's forgotten . . .

"I say! What's this I see? . . . In today's *Monde*. There must have been a leak. Look, that headline:

"'Important Paris publisher victim of joke in poor taste. Like the Bourgeois Gentilhomme speaking prose without knowing it, he brings out a "new" edition of a Prévost novel.'

"They say 'in poor taste,' but you can tell they're laughing, and they're not the only ones! Let's see what *Minute* and the *Canard enchaîné* have to say . . .

"April fool! Ever been had? To your very good health! . . ."

It seems watertight. What can Grouillot do? He's cornered. All he can do is shut up. My God, I'd give ten years of this dog's life I lead to see that!

One little vain regret in passing: my first indisputable masterpiece will remain almost as unknown as the soldier under the Arc de Triomphe. Fate is against me yet again. But I have no choice. The main thing is to get myself out of Grouillot's clutches at any price before he chokes me to death. I must concentrate on that agreeable thought.

As for plagiarism, my hands will be more or less clean. And Grouillot won't be getting the half of what he deserves.

As for good old Abbé Prévost, the happiness of being summoned back to life by a man of taste will make him overlook the matter of the borrowing. Anyway, he was familiar with that sort of thing in his own lifetime. An enormous proportion of seventeenth- and eighteenth-century French literature was published either anonymously or under a pseudonym, sometimes for reasons of political and erotic censorship, sometimes merely because gentlefolk would have thought it beneath them to put their name to an essay. And the hacks in those days never stopped helping themselves to other people's work.

Yes, the Abbé Prévost, wherever he is, couldn't but approve of my plans. Especially as he too has suffered at the hands of publishers. So he'll understand.

Thursday
March 8, 1973

There's a bone in my pâté de foie gras which I ought to have spotted sooner. The largest Prévost collection is certainly concentrated in the Bibliothèque nationale, which also has the equipment necessary for making reproductions. So I shall be more or less obliged to work there. And there Mlle Dubois is lurking like a spider in her web. What have I done to the Almighty that I should have such a woman on my back?

But we mustn't get excited unnecessarily. The Library is a universe in itself, and very departmentalized. Cécile's section has nothing to do with the quiet retreat where they keep, wrapped up in cotton wool, the unique volumes which are never lent but have to be consulted on the spot by permission of the librarian. And it's quite easy for me to get in there without being seen. Moreover, if by some chance Cécile heard I'd asked for photocopies of certain passages from Prévost, she'd still have to connect this apparently natural fact with the publication of my book.

What a fool I am! To avoid even this small risk, all I have to do is use a pseudonym and on some pretext or other insist that Grouillot take draconian measures to preserve my incognito. In this way I neutralize not only Cécile but also Mlle Grivas, the shortsighted bony fright who looks after the crucial section—everybody, in fact.

Still, it would be highly disagreeable to be caught. It's hard to imagine just how far the repercussions of such a scandal could go—there's no precedent. And justice has become a lottery that follows the unpredictable fluctuations of public opinion.

But why should it lead to a scandal even if someone were indelicate enough to make the connection? Human nature being what it is, the lucky sleuth would be more likely to hide his find under a bushel and try for as high a price as possible, and he would of course have to do business with Grouillot. In which case I wish the latter joy!

Anyway, here I am obliged to use a pseudonym once more! I shall never shake free of them—it's a vocation! But this time it won't be of any importance because (as a matter of course) the novel will be stillborn.

All this considered, the snag is not insurmountable. The Library isn't really a problem. If there's a danger it lies elsewhere. But where?

I admit I'm superstitious, a fault that becomes frequent whenever religion is in decline. And I can't help being struck by the celestial whim which puts the encyclopedia entry on

Prévost between one article on weather forecasting and another on prayer. Is this a hint on the part of Providence? If so, it's a tricky one to interpret.

Friday
March 9, 1973

This morning I went out for the first time since I caught cold, and I succumbed to the temptation of calling in at the Bibliothèque nationale. Spent two and a half hours on the catalogue of the Prévost collection, from which I've already taken a fair number of soundings. It's at the same time exciting and discouraging. It's like searching for a few drops of water in an ocean. It's certainly true that the least known and least published parts of the work are usually the least good. I think I'll have to take the best parts of two successive volumes, perhaps from *Les Mémoires et Aventures d'un homme de qualité*. There's also something to be got out of the *Mémoires d'un honnête homme*.

Of course the Christian names and surnames will have to be changed, and so will the place names. Every writer has his own characteristic topography. *Manon* is haunted by the ghost of the Saint-Lazare prison.

But if I use my judgment and take good care, I should be all right.

Mlle Grivas is translucent. For one moment I thought she was going to fly off the top of her ladder. Religion is a great resource for that sort of young woman: they turn into angels if they go up high enough. Her underskirt needs mending.

I took the opportunity to glance again at the Italian section, and in particular a few fragments of the correspondence of Casanova de Seingalt, the prudent adventurer who at the end of his life exclaimed, "I lived a philosopher, I die a Christian!" The best of both worlds.

There's a mystery about the life of Casanova. He caught pox after pox in the course of his busy amorous career, always leaping from bed to mercury bath, but died at the age of seventy-three, bright-eyed and bushy-tailed and lucid. Whereas most of the important French authors of the nineteenth century died ga-ga. In Prévost's day disease was an elixir. Under Napoleon III it played havoc with the republic of letters. Make what you can of it.

Saturday
March 10, 1973

Saw Cécile again in the Saint-Just lecture room, got up in a jersey dress that was too short. The familiar spell is broken. I have to make an effort now to catch her eye during the lecture. You can ask too much of a man! The business of the dedication, my cold, the umpteenth pseudonym that's forced on me —it's all beginning to have its effect! If I'm not careful I'll start to positively loathe her.

Exchanged a few politenesses with her at the end. Asked after Gustave. Carried heroism so far as to compliment her on the dress.

I'm bothered about what pseudonym to use. I'm tempted by the idea of an anagram of "Abbé Prévost." If things went wrong it would heighten the comical aspect of the scandal and might win over a few more people to see the joke. People would see it as taking a rather elegant risk—whereas in fact the risk is very small. How many readers would recognize Salvador Dali as "Avida Dollars"? It would be a piece of cake.

Bébert Sovap sounds too peculiar. But Béba Vesport has a certain charm, an aura of Central Europe and gypsies. And as Prévost was a monk at one time, I may as well adopt skirts. The few people who'll read it will be all the more delighted.

It occurs to me that for the few connoisseurs capable of appreciating it what I shall be producing will not be a pastiche in the usual sense of the term. A pastiche is usually based on one particular author, painter, sculptor, or composer, whereas I shall be thought to be doing a pastiche of a marvelous kind of language, which to me still sounds more alive than the language of today. But who will notice my exploit? How I'd have loved to revive Prévost for a legion instead of just a company!

More rain. If I were Simenon and had the gift of seeing

things instead of people (and even those I see in distorting mirrors), I'd be able to improvise without any effort one of those simple phrases that are so evocative. For example: "The rain was now drawing strange faces on the windowpanes . . ." There—at a stroke a connection is made between the elements and the inner world. What skill there at creating life, creating presence out of nothing.

As a matter of fact, the phrase is by Thomas Narcejac, doing a pastiche of Simenon in his book, *Usurped Identities*. But it is exactly like Simenon at his best and most rich. What a lesson for me!

Sunday
March 11, 1973

I fed Cécile at lunchtime in the rue du Cherche-Midi, at Dumonet's, one of the few places in Paris where they still do a superb meal at a reasonable price. I need to keep a close eye on that young woman.

She was in seventh heaven. I suppose she usually starves herself to feed the cat. I was horrified to hear how incredibly little she gets paid. The Bibliothèque nationale is a cruel stepmother. Towards the end of the meal I suggested she set fire to it, but she was worried about what would happen to the readers. She's full of the milk of human kindness. I was quite right to be worried.

As we came out of the restaurant I had a dazzling vision. Two charming young men were walking along the sidewalk in front of a big advertisement for washing powder, and all of a sudden I saw on the poster the words, "Omo-sexual washes whiter." That could be worth ten thousand dollars next year. We imaginative writers are always at it. All is grist that comes to our mill.

From the Diary of
Mademoiselle Cécile Dubois

3/12/73

Had lunch yesterday, Sunday, with Dominique, whose kindness is inexhaustible. What a delightful person! And so attentive, taking an interest in my time off as well as in my work.

Among other things we did justice to a "lou magret" cooked with sorrel—a sort of roast duck. It's so good you scarcely know what you're eating! The atmosphere, so calm and restful and distinguished, made a nice change after mass in Saint-Séverin, where I was stuck between the electric guitar and the barrel organ. I had some difficulty in following the service.

Dominique, unlike his wife, hasn't gone to mass for years. "You go to mass to communicate," he said. "I have such an imperishable memory of my first communion that I've never had the courage to do it again. I was afraid of being disappointed, afraid God might not turn up again. Anyhow, isn't one good dose of God enough for a lifetime? I like to think I've made my first and last communion. And anyway, in view of the risks you run nowadays of committing sacrilege, with all the disgraceful antics they get up to, it's much safer not to go at all!"

It's often hard to know how serious LL is. He's very baffling. He makes you think without apparently meaning to. He must know an awful lot.

We said good-bye after lunch. His time is precious.

Last night the couple who've just set up house together in the studio next door comported themselves without any regard for discretion. They're probably in the first flush of discovery. To get any peace at all I had to move the head of my bed away from the wall. Even then I tossed and turned . . .

I seem to remember dreaming that LL was dressed up as a

53

cat, like Jean Marais in *Beauty and the Beast*, and was running after me uttering untranslatable words and holding his striped trousers in his hand. That's certainly the last thing he'd do! He feels the cold terribly.

As I was setting off this morning for the Library, I passed the young woman next door in the corridor. She gave me a friendly smile, all innocence. For a moment I thought my memory must be playing tricks on me about last night. What is innocence?

From the Private File of
Labattut-Largaud

Monday
March 12, 1973

Went back to the Bibliothèque nationale like a duck to its pond. I think I've got hold of the recipe for my cocktail, mostly taken from the inexhaustible *Mémoires et Aventures d'un homme de qualité*. No shortage of incident in Prévost.

If I do decide to try my luck I shall have to risk inventing a few linking passages. And it wouldn't be a bad idea to antici-pate the reader with a foreword in which the mysterious Béba Vesport briefly explains her object in mixing anachronism and actuality. But I'll have to take good care that the style doesn't sound like either Prévost or myself. That should be feasible enough.

As for the title, I finally incline towards *Equivocations*. Am-biguity is Prévost's trademark, and recurs like a leitmotiv in the passages I've picked out at random as a test. (*L'Histoire d'une Grecque moderne* is positively startling in its ambiguity!) And that title would be all the more piquant in that the whole busi-ness is equivocal, to say the least!

I scent a completely unforeseen danger. Supposing *Equivocations* fell into the hands of some eminent expert in language, some shrewd connoisseur of the eighteenth century enjoying the well-earned leisure of retirement. There are still two or three in circulation who haven't yet got themselves run over.

Let's call this rare creature Pertinax for the sake of argument.

From the first pages of *Equivocations*, then, my Pertinax feels a vague uneasiness, which grows as he goes on: this is pure eighteenth century, and eighteenth century of the highest order. And the deeper Pertinax is drawn into the labyrinths of Prévost's characteristic psychology, the stronger becomes the impression of authenticity.

Now Pertinax knows perfectly well—though the general public does not—that even with the most scrupulous attention, the vastest erudition, and all possible and imaginable talents, no one can produce two or three hundred pages of exact and innocent pastiche out of a living language which has evolved with time. Sooner or later the author of the pastiche is bound to make mistakes which betray his own hand.

If *Equivocations* is altogether free of any clumsiness it isn't pastiche, it's plagiarism. Instead of being a skillful and ingenious fabrication in the antique fashion it's a borrowing from the past which a swindler has the audacity to present as his own work.

So who can be its real author?

Perhaps by combining all the means at the disposal of modern linguistics, comparative grammar, vocabulary, semantics, etymology, and so on, it is possible to narrow down a work by an anonymous author of the eighteenth century to within about a generation. That would depend, of course, on the length and nature of the work.

Then, as in the United States, the problem can be reduced still further by comparisons carried out with computers, which bring out the frequency of certain usages, repetitions, and other special characteristics.

If Pertinax carries his gratuitous meddling as far as that, I'm done for. After a few false starts he'll go straight to Prévost and blow up the whole thing.

So it's quite clear I must slip the necessary quota of "mistakes" and linguistic anachronisms into my *Equivocations* to make Pertinax think it's a highly successful pastiche. Dirty old man.

But it won't be easy! If my anachronisms are too crude he'll draw the obvious conclusion: i.e. "There's a contradiction between these mistakes and the general purity of style of the text. The same man couldn't be responsible for all of it. Some incompetent fraud has massacred this minor masterpiece to make people believe it's a pastiche."

On the other hand, some slight anachronisms in an overall context which is linguistically homogeneous place Pertinax before an insoluble alternative: either this is an exceptionally fine bit of plagiarism in which a connoisseur has given of his best or it's a plagiarism which a skillful crook has tricked up as a pastiche.

In case of doubt Pertinax probably wouldn't do anything about it.

Fortunately there's not one chance in a hundred thousand that I'll be dissected by a Pertinax. But competence is often more widespread than one thinks, and I'd prefer to have my mind really at rest on this point.

I'll take such precautions with Pertinax as he deserves. A few chosen grammatical anachronisms belonging to slightly before or slightly after the real period. But there are better and, if possible, more accurate weapons in the field of vocabulary. I'll fix up Pertinax with a few "foutaises" (poppycock). "Foutaise" isn't recorded earlier than 1790. And I'll stump him with "fric-frac" (burglary), which goes at least as far back as 1752. But I shan't let him have any "fox trots"!

Further discreet research and understandable hesitations at the Library, not to mention my Goethe symposium in Lucerne —my paper met with a very enthusiastic reception—have made me neglect my notebooks.

I have finally made my choice, and the day before yesterday Mlle Grivas handed over photocopies of the selection from which I shall be working. All this beavering away has been a great nuisance, but it has produced a body of material consistent within itself and extremely modern. It should bring success within a limited circle.

It might be effective to use eighteenth-century spelling— with a little inaccuracy here and there for Pertinax's benefit. Some forms current nowadays were used then only in poetry, for the sake of rhyme. In prose, too, when a present participle was used as an adjective the *t* at the end was left out before the *s* in the plural. "Un sentiment pressant" (an urgent emotion) became "des sentimens pressans." The word may have gained a letter over the years, but the thing itself has got lost in the process. The usual inflation.

It would be the polite thing to do to give Cécile another meal before the Easter vacation. I've racked my brains, but I just can't see how the blameless idiot can hurt me now. However, it never did any harm to be careful. I must keep an eye on Cécile till I'm out of the woods.

Afterwards a paradox will come into play that may give me some trouble. If you're seeing a young woman supposedly from no other motive than chaste friendship, there's no other motive either for ditching her. And the indifference of friendship is crueler than the indifference of love, for it wounds the whole being. When I've really had enough of her, I'll invent some quarrel to make it less hurtful. Like those husbands who are unfaithful with the nurse or the choirboy on their deathbeds, in the hope that their widows will feel less grief. In this wicked world the noblest acts of charity go unappreciated.

57

Spoke to Grouillot again yesterday, just in passing, about the idea for a super-rétro novel which he himself suggested. He only vaguely remembered. How frivolous can you get? Or was he afraid I might ask for an advance? That really is the limit. He seems to think now that his own idea was a rather risky one. After all the work I've put in! In the end he just said impatiently, as if he were expecting the Shah of Persia from one moment to the next, "Well, do it anyway and we'll see . . ." He didn't even say "I"! What a way to encourage an author who brought him the Grand Prix on a platter! If I ever get him where I want him I'll let him know it!

For an instant I felt discouraged. But may as well risk it. Put my trust in Prévost. And as Grouillot says, "We'll see."

As usual, we're going to La Claustraies for the Easter vacation—Easter is on April 22, and we'll be there from the sixteenth to the twenty-eighth. Better not be driving on Sunday, the fifteenth, and the twenty-ninth on those apocalyptic motorways bristling with guardian angels on motorcycles.

There on my nice refreshing lawn I'll have plenty of time to fake up my holiday task with plenty of crossings-out in the manner of Balzac to give an air of authenticity. What must be must be.

At the Library I saw a fragment of one of Prévost's manuscripts. There were hardly any crossings-out. But I'm only a follower, a pupil. I must be modest.

Reading the Abbé's handwriting gave me a slight pang. The old place at Claustraies on the edge of the forest of Senlis is not far from Courteuil, where Prévost met with a sudden death —the death of the holy or the damned. It's not superstitious to see the coincidence as a favorable omen. I'm more and more convinced that Prévost must be pleased with what I'm doing for him, and will collaborate to make it a success. Anyway . . . let's hope so.

Lunched with Cécile at La Méditerranée in the place de

l'Odéon. Despite the present ways of the world, she insists on abstaining on Fridays. What constancy! I put it to the test with a lobster au gratin, which she gobbled up in the midst of her remorse. Cheap at half the price!

Anyway, I was able to check that my recent comings and going at the Library haven't attracted her attention. And she told me there was no likelihood of her changing her job for some time. So it seems I'm covered from that angle too.

Mustn't forget to lock my notebooks up in the safe before we go away.

From the Diary of Mademoiselle Cécile Dubois

4/8/73

I missed mass this morning through dawdling—I still hadn't quite got over my indisposition of Friday evening. When I did get there, communion was over. Everyone was sitting looking at the ceiling, as if God was there and not in their stomachs. There's no getting away from it, something has changed in the Church, and it isn't always for the better.

I was punished for indulging in lobster on a Friday in Lent. But I couldn't refuse. Dominique took such pleasure in offering it . . . and it was so good! Dear Dominique! I sometimes wonder what he sees in me to make him so kind. It's true my conversation isn't entirely lacking in charm. I know quite a lot myself, though I learned it mostly from books rather than from life. But that could be just what interests him.

Still, I had a very disagreeable night afterwards. When it's not love that keeps me awake—if you can apply the word "love" to what goes on next door—then it's friendship!

Dominique leaves on the sixteenth for his house in the country, in his 1947 Citroën 15 CV. He promised me to be very,

very careful. I'm not at all easy in my mind to see him go off again in that ancient relic, despite his telling me he doesn't do as much as 3,000 kilometers in it a year, that it's as good as new, and that he takes great care of it in the hope that it'll be worth something in about fifteen years' time. That makes you wonder. And he hasn't even got a Saint Christopher medal. The vicar of Saint-Séverin is always going on about Saint Christopher and saying he never existed. He doesn't realize that's the best kind of saint in case of accident, because the time it takes them to intercede is a zero quantity.

It seems La Claustraies is an old mill surrounded by woods and fields, which Dominique converted into a second home after he won that Grand Prix writing under a pseudonym. I like to think of him in a country retreat where he can enjoy a well-earned rest in the bosom of his family.

The Senlis-Chantilly area is certainly very pretty. But it's a sort of literary graveyard. Rousseau died at Ermenonville all alone, having put his numerous offspring in orphanages, not from necessity but on principle! Prévost died at Courteuil one foggy day in November. He was all alone too. But he was a Benedictine, so children were less relevant.

Let's hope those distant precedents don't bring Dominique bad luck.

When he didn't see me at his lecture yesterday morning, he called up the concierge to inquire after me. She said something vague to the effect that I was all right—fortunately not mentioning indigestion. I think ours is developing into a really perfect friendship.

Since we've known each other better, Dominique pays less attention to me during his lectures. That's quite natural. Out of sight, in the mind!

One more lecture and then bon voyage, Dominique, till we meet again!

Meanwhile I'm moving into another section at the Library because of an affair of the heart. Poor Mlle Grivas has an unrequited passion for a cold-blooded fusspot of a librarian who scorns her in a perfectly shameful manner. You couldn't say hers is an exactly classical beauty, but that mild short-sighted look of hers, like a faithful hound, ought to win over any man of sensibility. The way she deliberately pined after that ungrateful wretch, she was bound to fall genuinely ill. She even managed to get thinner than she was before!

Friday afternoon, when the lobster was already beginning to disagree with me, Monsieur Lavergne called me into his office and asked me to take over from Mlle Grivas for a fortnight. It's a mark of trust and respect that he did so, but I don't like owing it to such an unhappy affair.

Gustave seems to have calmed down. Sometimes animals set us an example of wisdom and resignation.

If I still write in my diary from time to time, it's no longer out of the narcissism of adolescence, but in a sincere attempt to improve myself, especially when I read it over. And looking at the entry for March 12 last, I see I recounted a rather indecent dream—which I might well have omitted—and joked about LL running after me with his striped trousers in his hands when he feels the cold so. I seem to have forgotten, when I wrote that, how on February 26 he rode all the way across Paris on a motor bike, right in the middle of winter, in striped trousers and feeling the cold, to ask after my health. If he had read what I wrote he would have been very hurt.

One of the most useful rules of moral hygiene is to speak and write as if anyone, living or dead, could hear or read our words.

It is very difficult to be witty without being malicious at the same time. Though I haven't a lot of wit, I've still got too much. But the Holy Spirit protects us from the mind.

PART TWO

From the Private File of
Labattut-Largaud

Monday
April 30, 1973

Worked like a dog at La Claustraies. Never kept it up before at such a pace! I felt inhabited, transported, possessed by Prévost, who was grateful to me for doing better than he did, since I was correcting what he wrote!

Prévost himself, always persecuted either because of his own errors or because of other people's, rarely had the time to polish his work. His was a springing, torrential genius. Without detracting from his spontaneity and natural flow, I have channeled that genius slightly, sometimes adding more of myself than I expected. By cuts and additions—in fact, mostly cuts—I think I've produced the second *Manon* vouchsafed to him by fate. One hundred and ninety-nine pages of the first order.

I've often thought that great authors ought to be touched up and have their weak points improved by competent specialists. There's always something that needs doing.

Fortunately Claire and the children left me in perfect peace. For a long time now no one has taken the slightest interest, whatever I write. Goethe is above my nearest and dearest, and my nearest and dearest are above Battling Cassidy. I no longer exist, reduced to nothing between a genius that isn't mine on the one hand and on the other a genius I haven't got. It took Prévost to bring me back to life!

But coming back to the apartment, in which Maria-Dolores had let the dust accumulate, I suddenly lost all my enthusiasm. Perhaps because it's time for all the bills to come in.

I feel uneasy.

65

Last night Claire was snoring away beside me in her usual poetic manner. First the *grr-grr-grr* of a mouse gnawing a nut, then the little sigh of a child's balloon deflating. A bubble issued hesitantly from between her parted lips, accompanied by a deep though modest gurgle. The only way to stop her snoring is to make love to her. I have to choose between death from insomnia or from decline. By the time it's daylight I'm half sleepwalking and half dazed. How can anyone write in such conditions? At least at La Claustraies I had a room to myself.

Lying there in the dark, I went over in my mind all the factors in the problem, considering again, and as far as possible afresh, the certainties, the risks, and the hopes. By about five in the morning I was once more convinced I was right, and feeling reasonably optimistic. But my uneasiness was stronger than ever, somehow; I still had a sort of block. For the first time in my life I was about to do something seriously illegal, following in the footsteps of Battling Cassidy or La Reynière. It was a paralysis deeper than just a funk. I think it was all my bourgeois ancestors, rich or ruined, protesting.

In order to overcome my inertia I went over all the examples of adventure, honorable or dishonorable, offered by my forebears. Quite a number of them left the beaten track and threw themselves into uncommon dangers.

There was Louis-Amédée Labattut, guillotined in 1793 for speculating in oil. Charles Gustave, convicted in 1824 of fraudulent bankruptcy and abduction of a minor. Hyppolyte, a lawyer in Orléans, who fled to Brazil in 1848 with the money belonging to the diocese. Adolf, who disobeyed orders in 1871 and led his regiment into Switzerland rather than give dangerous and uncertain battle in country that was fertile. François Gérôme, who seduced his colonel's younger son, handed over to Italy the plans for a pneumatic corrector for the brakes of horse-drawn vehicles, and in 1887 broke the bank at Monte Carlo. There was Léon, a double agent, shot in Brussels in 1915 because of a mistake in the orders. Stanislas, professor of

Spanish at the University of Besançon, put on the retired list in 1939 for spreading anarchist propaganda. All of them took risks, dared.

And while I was stopping Claire from snoring for ten minutes, I was still thinking of the unfortunate Ambroise, lieutenant colonel in the 6th Engineers, shot down where he stood in the boulevard Bonne-Nouvelle in August 1944 by a drunken German trying to make him cross the road outside the pedestrian crossing.

Even on the Largaud side of the family there were a few little crooks and one dubious hero.

I got up and tossed for it, heads or tails, by the light of the little lamp by the side of the bed. Adventure won.

A little while before noon, after one last hesitation, I delivered the manuscript to Grouillot's, handing it over to the caretaker on duty for the May Day holiday.

It'll get a resentful reading, anyhow. Another bone of contention between me and Grouillot is that he likes manuscripts to be typed. But I can't type and have no intention of learning. The machine horrifies me—it would simply dry up my natural flow. And as good secretaries are rare and cost the earth, and as neither Grouillot nor I am prepared to pay the earth, it's stalemate.

But it's an ill wind . . . For once a handwritten manuscript will lend an added air of authenticity. The hand deceives better than any instrument. And alas, the heart deceives even better than the hand!

From the Diary of
Mademoiselle Cécile Dubois

5/5/73

Dominique seems absent, tense, preoccupied, as if his holiday hadn't done him any good. At the end of the lecture this morning he greeted me with nothing better than commonplaces. What's bothering him?

Mlle Grivas got hurt in a May Day demonstration, and has been given another week off. The poor girl was out buying a loaf of bread and a slice of ham, and got sandwiched herself between two streams of fanatics. There couldn't have been much of her left. I must go and see how she is.

5/6/73

After mass—this time I tried Notre-Dame: where is one to go to be able to pray in peace?—I walked to Mlle Grivas' pied-à-terre behind the Arènes de Lutèce.

It's very nicely furnished, with souvenirs from Catalonia—she's a refugee from there. She won't go back until after Franco's death, an event she's been awaiting eagerly ever since she was born. She's a passionate advocate of independence for Catalonia, in which she would include French Catalonia. I've always thought she rather went to extremes.

Anyhow, she isn't too bad—she's only got a sprained ankle. She was very grateful to me for coming to see her, and gave me an extremely warm welcome. She really is a very nice person.

As she still limped rather badly I went out and bought her some paella, and we ate it together.

During our snack she entrusted me with some modest confidences on her unhappy love affair. It's very sad. She needed someone to talk to.

And so by chance I learned that before the vacation LL was doing some research on two volumes in the Prévost collection, and that he took away whole sheaves of photocopies. I don't remember having seen him at the Library then, but stranger still, he hasn't told me he was doing a lot of work on Prévost. Though of course there's nothing out of the way in that, in itself. You couldn't say it shows mistrust. Anyway, what does it matter? But it's very strange.

However, since he hasn't thought fit to speak to me about it, it's not for me to introduce the subject.

In the afternoon, paid an interesting visit to the Musée

Guimet with Tra-duc-Ho, a young Vietnamese chap, very quiet and polite, who moves and speaks almost noiselessly. By common consent we avoided politics. He says he's a Buddhist of the Little Vehicle. He added, laughing silently, "The tiny one, the purest!" He told me, rather to my surprise, that Buddha was an atheist. According to Tra-duc-Ho, the West will never understand Buddhism until it has renounced its appetites and desires. "Even the desire for God?" I asked. "Especially the desire for God," he said, "because that's the most ardent of all!"

At all events, he won't embarrass me with his attentions. He doesn't look ardent enough for that!

From the Private File of
Labattut-Largaud

Monday
May 14, 1973

After spending a fortnight on hot coals, torn between fear of rejection and dread of success, I received this morning by hand (Grouillot has almost given up trusting anything to the post—it plays him such dastardly tricks) the indescribable letter which I set down here as precious and prodigious evidence of malice pure and simple. '

Félix Grouillot   May 14, 1973
to Dominique Labattut-Largaud

Dear Friend:
    As the literary season is getting on, we have done our best to reach a decision as soon as possible on *Equivocations*, most of which we eventually managed to decipher.
    The select reading committee and I for once come to the same conclusion.

The book certainly has its attractive aspects: a very felicitous and flowing style; a classically strong plot with unexpected twists; a psychology which is complex without being artificial, and the ins and outs of which are highly intriguing. Fabricius is a very human character, Clélie very touching. Even minor characters such as the Marchioness of Oxbridge, Barneveld the financier, and Aïssa, the maid from Ragusa, are real and three-dimensional. The triangular circuit between Paris and Amsterdam, Amsterdam and London, returning finally to Paris, ever in search of ever-fleeing pleasure and happiness, we found very taking.

On the other hand, I shall not attempt to conceal the fact that we were much less drawn by the insistence on archaism, historical reconstruction (which even goes so far as to include spelling!), a sort of leaning towards "rétro," in short, which seems to us to be carried too far. By summoning up all the resources of your unequaled learning, you have given us an authentic eighteenth-century novel of such high quality that the present gets quite lost. We are afraid the more enlightened public will see it not so much as an original work but as a tour de force, more of a collector's piece than a living novel relevant to modern sensibility. You probably aimed too high—perhaps the specialist in you got the better of the novelist, who needed only the opportunity to give full expression at last to his extraordinary force and talent.

I do not forget, however, that it was I myself who suggested an attempt of this kind. But what I had in mind was a mere whiff of the eighteenth century, whereas this brilliant and overperfect pastiche is impregnated with a whole flaskful of the most pungent odors. No one regrets the misunderstanding more than I do. I frankly admit I didn't know what you were capable of!

We sincerely regret that our desire to afford you every opportunity in a field more exciting than the one in which you usually operate has not produced—

admittedly because of its very distinction—a work more obviously suited to the present-day mood.

The foreign pseudonym strikes me as pointless, and we are all of the opinion that the introduction would do more harm than good, underlining as it does the tour de force aspect of the performance. Moreover, the style in which the introduction is written is less easy than that of the book itself, as if, on consideration, you felt weighed down by the burden of your own success.

In short, we do not think that at the present time *Equivocations* could command the wide audience it deserves.

However, a gap in our schedule, due to a death and to an unforeseen lawsuit of which you have no doubt heard, has made us decide nevertheless to bring the book out very shortly in an edition of 3,500 copies in our semi-luxury series, "Sign of the Times."

Very cordially yours, etc.

Disgusting! In the normal way publishers always begin that sort of letter with a phrase that puts the author out of his misery straightaway—"It gives me great pleasure . . ." or, "I am sorry to have to tell you . . ." Grouillot obviously took a sadistic pleasure in finessing right to the end of the last sentence. He's a monster—he deserves to publish two *Equivocations* rather than one, to flood the civilized world with them, to his eternal shame! Anyway, I've got him where I want him!

The social unrest of May '68 left me with personal memories that were disagreeable rather than otherwise. I now realize rather late in the day that those dreadful upheavals had an appealing, human side. For example, there was Grouillot shut up in his office for three days by jubilant strikers and reduced to munching his own cigars. Grouillot roughed up and quivering like jelly, threatened with being chucked out of the window into the rue Monsieur-le-Prince four floors below! And then they went and botched it and let him go! The people are too kindhearted. They'll regret it.

Phoned Grouillot towards the end of the morning to say how grateful I was and insist about the incognito. I said I suffered from Freudian disturbances and superstitious nervousness because of the failure of *Resurgences*, the only work published up till now under my own name.

Grouillot wasn't unduly surprised. Ever since Freud it's been much easier to pass oneself off as a nut. He's a gift for innocents and crooks.

Anyhow, I see freedom flying towards me on the wings of just revenge! I'm overjoyed!

Friday
May 18, 1973

Strange to think *Equivocations* might have missed the boat if it hadn't been for the gap in the production schedule caused by Bernouville's sudden demise.

Grouillot usually takes at least three months to bring out one of my books, but this hole in the program has speeded things up incredibly for once. Editing, scheduling, sending out, printing, distribution—the conveyor belt must be kept going as far as possible all the time. So as Grouillot had already given the printer a date, he's using me as a stopgap.

I'll have the proofs by the end of the month, and they're already talking about the jacket design. To save time we've given up the idea of commissioning something original. Grouillot fancies something smutty, a detail from Fragonard or Boucher —he tried to sell me a pair of period buttocks that bear a striking resemblance to his own face. I'd prefer a more ethereal Watteau.

One of Bernouville's many peculiarities was that he set himself up as an expert on Saint-Simon, whom he didn't like and therefore didn't understand. We had a row about it once at a conference in Florence. I can't bear these busybodies who fabricate pseudoculture for barbarians.

Anyway, there's not much more to be said about Saint-Simon since Monsieur Judrin dealt with him. I can still remember the beginning of his article in the Encyclopedia universalis: "The encounter between Louis XIV and Saint-Simon is unique in the annals of literature. The ingredients were a great king not entirely a tyrant and a great observer, almost unknown, who was such a born writer he did not care whether he was known or not." And this prodigy of wit goes on for five solid columns, as if through some osmosis of sympathy and talent Monsieur Judrin were writing with Saint-Simon's own pen and expressing at the same time his hero and himself.

I've got a weak spot for Saint-Simon. He used to keep note-books too—for sixty years!

It's about time I made another polite gesture to Cécile. For the last couple of Saturdays she's been giving me rather hungry smiles.

My policy there is to maintain a delicate balance. If I leave long enough intervals she'll soon forget me and her natural curiosity will wear off—but that means I can't be keeping an eye on her. On the other hand, if I pay her too much attention it might act as a dangerous stimulant to that female chartist's perspicacity of hers.

I try to get around the problem by leaving intervals of just the right length. I hate going to trouble for nothing.

I know it all sounds horribly mean and degrading and Machiavellian. But telling lies is wrong only when it does harm, and all I'm trying to do is protect my own legitimate interests with the irreducible minimum of grace. There's nothing for me to feel guilty about.

I've always regarded myself as a tenderhearted sort of person whose bark is worse than his bite, and I'm not going to start being nasty now. Grouillot is an awful warning!

From the Diary of
Mademoiselle Cécile Dubois

5/19/73

LL seemed in great form this morning in the Saint-Just lecture room: relaxed, self-assured, soon sparkling with amusing digressions. In a word, transformed! His sensitiveness makes him very volatile. Unfortunately it wasn't long before I had fresh proof of it.

After the lecture Dominique very kindly asked me to lunch again, and we took a taxi to Dumonet's, where the food was as excellent as ever. "True cooks are born, not made," as poor Mama used to say every time she burned the joint.

What with the effects of the burgundy, plus the fact that I found LL's deviousness rather irritating, I couldn't help referring to Prévost. It was risky and indiscreet and not very kind, but so far no real damage was done.

LL obviously found the subject unpleasant and tried to change it, but I very unwisely kept it up.

I don't know what demon was driving me on, but I airily asked him whether he mightn't be thinking of taking a closer interest one day in Prévost: *Manon* was translated into German a few years ago by Lernet-Holenia. LL said at once that it was right outside his field—Prévost died before Goethe was fifteen years old.

I ought to have been ashamed, provoking an upright and estimable man like that to tell lies—especially if, as I should like to think, the secret is perfectly respectable. But at the time I was cross with his way of going about it, as if it showed lack of trust, as if LL were in the slightest degree accountable to me!

And just as he was about to tuck into the pink juicy flesh of a nice, crisp, delicious-smelling saddle of lamb, I carried my indescribable pestering further, idly alluding to the fact that I'd been switched to another section, mentioning my new duties and adding that the unforeseen situation would be prolonged now that Mlle Grivas had gone into a sanatorium in the Pyrénées for observation.

At the very first words my poor Dominique, who's very bad at dissimulating when he's really upset, choked on a mouthful and started to go to pieces before my very eyes.

I realized, now it was too late, that I'd have done much better to keep quiet. I didn't know what to do with myself.

LL made an effort to pull himself together.

"I'm very sorry to hear it," he said. "I mean, that Mlle Grivas is ill. I had occasion to appreciate her kindness and efficiency when I was working on some Italian manuscripts last December. We got on very well together. I can see myself now, holding the ladder for her . . ."

Embarrassing! So then it was I who attempted to change the subject, while LL kept trying to wrest it back again somehow, like a lark hypnotized by a mirror. He went on beating about the bush, but the object of all these maneuvers was quite plain: Did I or did I not know about his recent visit and the photocopies he'd had made?

Unfortunately, as he didn't dare ask the question outright and I didn't dare give an explanation offhand that might have finished him off altogether, the only way this awful conversation could end was in exhaustion on both our parts.

When the meal was finished LL got up, green in the face, and went and shut himself in the washroom, where no doubt, because of my imprudence and ingratitude, he threw up all the lunch to which he'd just invited me. I could have kicked myself!

But still, what's all the mystery about? What can LL be doing that's so hush-hush with those extracts from two volumes of the "Amsterdam edition, published at the Company's expense"? It doesn't make sense! Oh, how upset I am, and how intrigued!

Prévost is so much on my mind that this afternoon I read the preface to the "10/18" paperback edition of *L'Histoire d'une Grecque moderne*.

I'd found the novel itself interesting when I read it, though it is written in a less easy style than that of *Manon*. It's as if the writing suffered from the endless complications of the plot: you can never make out the real subjective truth about the characters. There's complexity everywhere—subtle and controlled complexity, but it soon gets rather tiring.

I learned from the preface that Prévost based his heroine, Théophé, on the Circassian princess Aïssé, who was bought as a slave by Louis XIV's ambassador in Istanbul. He brought her back to France, where she became known through her correspondence with the Chevalier Blaise Marie d'Aydie. When I say she became known, I mean she achieved great but short-lived notoriety. Who's ever read Aïssé nowadays? Or heard of her natural daughter, Célénie? And yet what a strange fate was hers, this slave transported from the harems of Turkey to the high society of Paris! And what talent she had! Some of her letters express the extravagances of passion with a force and felicity I can still remember.

I shall always have felt other people's passions instead of my own.

From the Private File of Labattut-Largaud

Tuesday
May 22, 1973

My presentiments did not deceive me. Mlle Dubois was brought into this world especially to plague me. And the worst of it is, I can't even make out if she really knows or not. During that wretched lunch last Saturday she sometimes looked as open and innocent as ever, but sometimes I thought I discerned a disconcerting artfulness. And that's as far as I can get!

I'm not a very good observer—I'm too absorbed in the spectacle that I present myself. But Cécile is observant by nature, the way children are. And she noticed I was shocked and perturbed.

I'd probably have done better to admit right away that I was interested in Prévost and given some ordinary explanation that would have lulled any suspicion she might feel. Too late to think of that now.

But one thing is reassuring—I can't see any reason why she should go comparing *Equivocations* with the two fateful volumes. Grouillot publishes a good thirty books a month. Why should she take it into her head to read *Equivocations* rather than another? And even if she did, there's nothing to link Béba Vesport and myself, or the book itself and Prévost.

All that's quite reasonable and sensible. But is life reasonable and sensible? I'm scared.

Friday
May 25, 1973

I've just received the proofs of *Equivocations*. I felt the usual slight pang, though more pronounced than usual.

Rushed work, full of mistakes. And the author's the last person to be able to correct it efficiently. It's well known that we don't take in each individual character, only constructions and sequences of syllables. And we tend to skim, because we've written the sentences ourselves and know them by heart. In this instance the text isn't literally mine, but I copied it so closely it amounts to the same thing.

But I have to go through with the boring task—the book can't be passed for press without the writer's authorization. And by putting my signature I'll be explicitly assuming responsibility for the deception.

For the cover I've persuaded them to use a charming, misty reproduction of Watteau's "Embarquement pour Cythère." But I've cut the introduction. Grouillot can sometimes be right on his own ground.

But I'm sorry to lose the last couple of sentences, which in the circumstances were very apt:

"So a man of quality has tried to write for the man of virtue. Since those virtues are ageless, may this book remain ever young."

I thought Cécile looked very downcast at my lecture on the twenty-fifth. I bet she knows. The very sight of her made me feel queasy—I could hear again the plaintive bleat of the sacrificial saddle of lamb.

Whatever I say, Chantal will keep on wearing trousers. They make her behind look enormous, and now that the weather's warmer there isn't even any excuse. She says skirts are immodest and that when her mother sits down carelessly she "shows everything she's got." There's no denying that.

But trousers are still in question. There are two kinds of girls nowadays—those who wear skirts out of brazenness and those who wear pants out of pride, so as not to play a feminine role, so as to escape the immemorial modesty and passivity that have always been the crowning glories of the fair sex. But you can live to regret being brazen, and as for pride, when the whole of society goes in for it, it's an incurable disease—and doesn't exclude the worst kind of lechery once the pants are down. Chantal is off to a bad start.

But François still finds work comes easily. He's like me there. In another twenty years he'll be writing first-rate pastiches.

Equivocations will soon be coming out. I find it hard to control my anxiety, and have to take orange-flower water to make me sleep. I prefer to steer clear of artificial aids—they get you into bad habits. I sleep better as a result, but my dreams are more agitated than usual and Claire's always waking me up to interview me. Last night I had to explain some characters out of Prévost that I'd given borrowed names, such as Clélie and Aïssa. No point in telling Claire about the pastiche—and still less about the plagiarism!

I'm quite pleased with myself for calling my Ragusan maid Aïssa, the Arabic form of the Turkish Aïssé, in honor of the letter writer of that name who died young in about 1740. It sounds very eighteenth century. But Pertinax is the only one who'll see the connection and appreciate me.

I have a vague feeling I've read something during the past year or so about Mlle Aïssé. Perhaps it was in some reference book. It's of no importance.

Cécile still looked down in the mouth at this morning's lecture. Like a chef's dog that's got lost and comes back to find the kitchen door shut. But she can't cook up any more trouble for the moment. I'll whistle her up again when the situation's changed.

She alternates between trousers and dresses that show powder-pink panties. It's either a sign of good equilibrium or else she subconsciously combines pride with lechery.

From the Diary of
Mademoiselle Cécile Dubois

6/17/73

The vicar-general preached about the Larzac affair, in which the farmers are fighting to save their land from the army, which wants to extend its field for maneuvers. He came out gently but firmly against the army, and encouraged the farmers to adopt a policy of passive resistance. I remember one typical sentence: "If resistance is forced to arise in the heart of a people, it must express itself in nonviolence, at first instinctive and then brought to perfection by practice." He reminds me of my friend Tra-duc-Ho, who told me he once thought of burning himself alive in order to impress everyone.

The vicar-general always likes the congregation to enter into a dialogue, so an elderly gentleman wearing medal ribbons got up and said, "You should have given that sermon to the Resistance in 1944! I was one of them. It's too late to preach cowardice now. Why do you do it—because the enemy's changed?"

This sarcasm unleashed a general outcry, followed by the beginnings of fisticuffs between the violent and the less violent. My efforts to soothe the people around me were vain. Communion had to be put off to another time. Deplorable.

I shall try Saint-Geneviève next Sunday.

LL is cold-shouldering me, and with reason. After several

Saturdays of comparative indifference he didn't turn up at all yesterday for the last lecture of the course. Perhaps he's ill. But this time I don't like to inquire.

How could I behave so stupidly? I must admit LL's attentions gave me more pleasure than I would have thought possible. They gave every appearance of the most natural and flattering disinterestedness. And I went and spoiled it all! I deserve to be left all on my own, without a friend and without communion.

The written exams are on June 19 and 20. The oral's at the beginning of July. Shall I see LL then? Dominique.

From the Private File of Labattut-Largaud

??

Weak as I am, I've managed to drag myself to my desk to try to bring things up to date. For what seems an endless length of time I've been vegetating, beset with sweet dreams and horrible nightmares.

I must go slowly and try to be accurate. My head feels as if it's stuffed with cotton wool.

On Wednesday, June 13, walking past the Palais de Chaillot at about five in the afternoon, I was suddenly struck with a strange sensation of cold—my teeth started to chatter as if I'd been seized with an attack of flu or malaria. I don't know how I got back to the rue de la Pompe—fortunately it's quite near. For more than a week I've had a raging fever, with bouts of delirium but no other particular symptoms. During a lucid interval I heard the family doctor, Chavanon, diagnosing "influenza, pure and simple." His prescriptions proved his words.

And then on Friday, June 22, when the fever had left me completely exhausted, what did I hear but Chavanon breezily diagnosing—subject to the usual tests—a case of infectious hepatitis. By way of consolation he told me it was very fashionable and that he was a specialist in it at the American Hospital in Neuilly.

Sure enough, starting with the whites of my eyes, which were what had given the alarm, I started to go yellower and yellower all over. My tongue was coated with white, and I produced stools like those of a Pekingese. Blood and urine tests confirmed the presence of A-type viral hepatitis in a form somewhat more than usually severe.

It was explained to me that the most up-to-date French and American medical practice knew of only three effective remedies against this visitation: Neapolitan idleness, evangelical fasting, and the warmth of the family hearth. I was a prisoner for weeks.

Every so often I'd have a feeling that something important was afoot, but I couldn't remember exactly what it was. From the twenty-fifth onwards my eyes must have got clearer, and on Wednesday, the twenty-seventh—a fortnight after the beginning of the attack—Claire decided I was well enough to appreciate a piece of good news and feel the better for it.

I could tell that Claire, who'd been sleeping in Chantal's room, was getting ready to make a revelation of some importance. She kept fussing around my bed with the embarrassed look I remembered from years ago, when she confessed to a unique unfaithfulness (repeated eleven times, however) performed with a young architect who lived on the ground floor while I was in Lisbon expatiating to a distinguished audience on the sufferings of young Werther.

And sure enough she leaned over me and said, "You really are incredibly lucky, darling! Wait till I tell you! They're going to make a big film in color of your *Equivocations*. And that's not all. Listen . . ."

I gave a groan and dived under the bedclothes. Claire thought I'd expired with joy.

To put it in a nutshell—I'm already exhausted with writing —*Equivocations* was launched, much against the grain, on June 15, a Friday, the smart day for visiting museums.

By the twentieth Grouillot had got rid of 1,350 copies and

sales were falling off. (A pleasant change from *Resurgences*, which never sold more than 423. Some people have talent and some don't.)

On the same day, on the plane from Paris to Rome, Mag Bodard, whose taste for the eighteenth century was not, it seems, exhausted by *Benjamin*, glanced through our—my—the novel, and phoned Grouillot from Fiumicino airport to ask if the rights were free.

The only possible explanation of this heavenly miracle is an express intervention on the part of the Abbé Prévost, presumably only recently let out of purgatory. The very fact that, with the couldn't-care-less-ness of Italy on the one hand and the shambles of France on the other, the telephone actually worked is a strikingly supernatural event in itself.

On the twenty-first, Mag Bodard, having returned from Rome without proceeding to the deserts of Arabia, bought the rights for 27,000 francs. The lowness of the figure must have made her purchase outright rather than just take an option. An unknown author using a pseudonym and published in a few thousand copies is bound to be cheap. (How was Mag to know that even what she paid was too dear, and that she could have got the book for nothing at the Bibliothèque nationale!)

As I was still delirious, that greedy traitor of a Grouillot, despite all his assurances, spilled the beans to Claire, who remembered she had power of attorney and lost no time in signing the contract on my behalf.

Put up to it by Grouillot, she for once had enough sense not to tell the children, who would have told Maria-Dolores, who would have told Toby, and so on and so forth. Ever-loving offspring prefer to keep mum about Dad's failures, but trumpet forth his usurped success. They'll believe anyone, even a father presumptive.

Grouillot, for his part, rejoiced sincerely in his modest good fortune. (By the terms of the unconscionable contract I have with him, he cheats me out of a mere 50 percent of the "subsidiary rights"—film, translation, etc.—just for sitting there and twiddling his fat greasy thumbs. This sort of highway robbery doesn't exist in the United States—American authors aren't such nitwits.)

The critics couldn't get out of mentioning *Equivocations* as it was going to be made into a film. Quite a number must actually have leafed through it. The most conscientious may even have read it.

As the talented Mag Bodard is one of the last producers to keep the canoe of the French cinema afloat, it would be treason against the national economy to question her choices. So the notices of *Equivocations* have been on the whole excellent. Even *France-Soir* hasn't found any errors in the registration this time, and has been publishing all sorts of tidbits about it.

On Sunday the twenty-fourth, Cardinal Daniélou, member of the French Academy, told a repentant adulteress the book was full of examples to be avoided, and recommended it to adult readers of suitable experience.

By the twenty-seventh, when Claire put me in the picutre, the first printing was sold out and another 18,000 copies were ordered from the printer.

On the twenty-eighth Roger Peyrefitte maliciously alleged that *Equivocations* was by the unfortunate Cardinal himself, and said he was pushing it in order to get more proceeds for charity.

On the thirtieth the Cardinal issued a denial, taking cover behind the confidentiality of the confessional.

On July 4 another 30,000 copies were ordered.

On the same day the provincial of the Jesuits published a denial, which by yet another miracle was believed.

The pseudonym now worked in the book's favor. People bought it in order to try to guess who'd written it. Bets were laid in fashionable drawing rooms.

From July 4 onwards Grouillot launched quite a good publicity campaign, stressing the spicy and mysterious aspects of the product. Grouillot's motto is: "In the mass media publicity should accompany sales rather than precede them." Then he winks and adds under his breath, "With mass mediocrities the carrot should accompany the stick."

Between the fourth and the tenth the book sold 26,000 copies.

On the eleventh Grouillot decided to print another 75,000,

to supply Paris up to the holiday exodus and then cater to the provinces during August.

So this is—let me think—July 14. So far fraud must have brought me in more than 200,000 francs, and as Claire said when she told me about my devil's own luck, "That's not all!" With every hour that passes the theft reaches new proportions.

"Time, steal away no more," as the sensitive and virtuous Lamartine said on his Lake while he licked the kids, I mean kissed the lids—Lord, I'm exhausted—of dreamy Monsieur Charles's consumptive spouse. But Lamartine, even with an intemporal lapse, couldn't steal all the time. When it came to unscrupulousness he was a mere child compared with me, the yellow Stakhanovite!

God, what shall I do, what shall I do? I can't bear it. I'm going crazy.

In my present plight my thoughts naturally turn to Cécile and the pleasant memories we have in common. I realize now that it's too late that the friendship I felt for her may have been something more. This evening I sorely miss her charming presence. Cécile! Why have you neglected me for so long? I'd love to hear your wise voice again and try to read the verdict in your eyes, so severe and yet sometimes so gentle. I need your advice badly.

From the Diary of
Mademoiselle Cécile Dubois

6/21/73

The written exam went off without incident yesterday and the day before. They told me in the office at the Faculty of Letters that LL has been quite seriously ill and may not attend the oral on July 6. I would have been upset if he'd happened to be my examiner, but I'd have been glad to see that he was better. Rumor has it he's had flu, with complications.

I do hope it wasn't made worse by any worry I may have caused him.

Saw a billboard in the subway that said, "Your cat has the same problems as you." It was an ad for a diet for fat cats that don't get enough exercise. At first I thought it referred to something else.

6/29/73

Aïssa, Aïssé, what are you doing in all this?!

I've just read Béba Vesport's *Equivocations*, which everyone's talking about, and I can't help having horrible suspicions . . .

But let me try to think calmly. The author has a marvelous knowledge of the eighteenth century—like LL. He's probably an academic—like LL. The book's published by Grouillot—who publishes LL. And LL has been taking a very suspicious interest in Prévost.

But I'd never have brought all these coincidences together if one final coincidence hadn't thrown a sudden shaft of light—if I hadn't been brought up short at the name Aïssa, which reminded me of *L'Histoire d'une Grecque moderne*.

If LL has been plagiarizing it's easy to see how he came to make such a slip. Every eighteenth-century specialist has at least heard of Mlle Aïssé's letters. But only the few who are specialists in Prévost—and LL's not one of them—could know that Prévost based his heroine Théophé on her. This minor point of literary history was revealed only in the preface to the recent paperback edition of the *Grecque*. LL might have read the novel without looking at the preface, or even read the preface and not paid any particular attention. If, afterwards, he was tempted to plagiarize, the *Grecque* and *Manon* would in fact, by the nature of the case, be the only two books by Prévost he wouldn't have to bother with. And when he was trying to think up an Oriental-sounding eighteenth-century name for his Dalmatian maid he might quite naturally have chosen Aïssé, if only as proof of his competence in the period. Too competent

85

by half on the one hand and not competent enough on the other!

It makes me feel quite ill to think of going and checking up on it all tomorrow morning!

Went to mass at an unearthly hour in the Benedictine church in the rue de la Source. It was scarcely daylight. I was in need of comfort, and it's come in handy since I read *Equivocations* this evening. The Latin plain chant did me good. And they have mass there on Fridays as well as Sundays.

6/30/73

I feel quite sick. He really did do it. He really was capable of such a thing. And he sank to the lowest kind of evasion and trickery in the process. A fine piece of work!

It's such a blow. So absurd as to be unbelievable. So different from all I know of him, all I imagined, all I felt. Can one really be so mistaken about someone? How can factual truth clash so cruelly with the truth of the heart? It's incredible. I just can't believe it.

But the evidence is indisputable and overwhelming. There's no escape.

And now that the danger's over it would be ungrateful of me not to give thanks to Providence. I almost fell in love . . . perhaps I did fall in love (why not admit it now?) with a man who didn't exist.

What a narrow escape! What sort of life would I have had with someone capable of plagiarizing Prévost? In retrospect I tremble at the thought.

Thank you, God.

Sunday
July 1

I really don't see what I could say or write to LL. We're suddenly beyond words.

But I can't let such a scandal continue. That viper Peyrefitte has attributed *Equivocations* to Cardinal Daniélou. That's too much!

There's one person above all the rest who ought to be told. I'll write to him something like this:

Mlle Cécile Dubois to Monsieur Félix Grouillot
PERSONAL
STRICTLY CONFIDENTIAL

Dear Sir:

I work as an assistant librarian at the Bibliothèque nationale, and it is my duty to inform you of a discovery that by an extraordinary chance I have recently made: *Equivocations*, by Monsieur Labattut-Largaud, is plagiarized from two volumes by the Abbé Prévost published in "the Amsterdam edition, at the Company's expense." Not so much as 10 percent of the text can even be called pastiche. You will also observe that the name Béba Vesport is an obvious anagram of "Abbé Prévost."

It is only natural that you, the chief victim of this indescribable deception, should be the first to be informed. You will know better than I what must be done to put an end to it as soon as possible, in order to protect the interest of the public and as far as possible your own.

Yours with sincere regrets, etc.

Bought Gustave a collar and leash and gave him an airing in the hallway to get him used to being led. Next Sunday we'll try to find some quiet square.

7/10/73

Passed the oral with special mention, not undeserved in view of the terrible ordeal I've been going through.

I've been so weak as to put off posting the letter to Monsieur Grouillot. I'll do it tomorrow.

87

Nearly lost Gustave last Sunday. I took him in his basket to stretch his legs in the Parc de Montsouris, and he ran up a chestnut tree and almost strangled himself in his leash. I was so frightened I almost forgot LL for a few minutes!

From the Private File of Labattut-Largaud

Monday
July 16, 1973

No doubt about it, I'm getting better. Chavanon thinks that by next week, if the elevator isn't out of order, I could risk going out for first time and go and buy a box of matches at the tobacco shop across the road. I still feel weak, but I think my mind is working better and tires less easily. Chavanon says that between now and when I go out I can have some oil on my salad. What a purist. I've lost twenty-three pounds and I wasn't any too fat before.

Claire still sleeps in Chantal's room. I'm allowed oil now but not Claire. According to Chavanon, the briefest imprudence in that respect might lay me low.

I passed on to the hepatitis expert, who was very touched, Grouillot's flagons of Chivas and Davidoff. They were only cluttering up the place, and were as good as an attempt at premeditated murder.

What can that bluestocking Cécile be up to? Anyhow, if she'd ferreted anything out she'd have lost no time in letting me know.

Be that as it may, I must put off all crucial and crucifying decisions until I'm surer of my strength and of my ability to see things straight. My reactions are not agile enough in my present state.

A nice juicy article by old Biquet-Lagravelle in the *Review of*

Comparative Grammar, in which he shrewdly accuses Béba Vesport of a few minor inconsistencies. Some of his remarks are hair-raisingly perceptive, though there's no hint about plagiarism. But for how long?

Now that *Equivocations* is spreading like wildfire it seems inevitable that sooner or later the deception will be found out. It's difficult to calculate the extent exactly, but there's no doubt wide distribution increases the risk. But what can I do?

I must do something to take my mind off things. To loosen myself up I'll write Grouillot my first letter as a convalescent.

Dominique Labattut-Largaud to Félix Grouillot
July 16, 1973
CONFIDENTIAL

My dear friend:

As my strength and faculties gradually return, I am making certain disagreeable discoveries about the way my interests were looked after during the few weeks when illness prevented me from being responsible for them myself.

I realize you could not have foreseen the startling success of *Equivocations*. It is outside your usual range. Everyone knows the case of Servan-Schreiber's *American Challenge,* of which 20,000 copies were printed with the utmost hesitation, and which had a smash hit I needn't remind you of, inexplicable though it still remains. To err is human.

But was it really necessary to let Mag Bodard acquire for such a derisory sum a highly original work which could have brought in six times as much if you'd only waited? My wife's inexperience is no excuse—it only increases your own responsibility.

You will easily understand that I find it increasingly difficult to remain with a publisher who seems to be wholly devoted to improvidence and amateurism.

When my health is fully restored we must have a frank and friendly talk about all this.

Yours, etc.

That'll please him!

From the Diary of
Mademoiselle Cécile Dubois

7/18/73

When I came home today to give Gustave his lunch and make a light snack for myself, I was informed by the concierge that a person she suspects of being from a private detective agency had called to make inquiries about me. It could only have been Grouillot, and it's extremely indelicate of him.

This morning he must have got the note I finally brought myself to post yesterday evening. He certainly hasn't wasted any time.

7/19/73

Today I received a few brief but very friendly lines from Monsieur Grouillot, asking me to be good enough to call at his office in the rue Monsieur-le-Prince and go and dine with him. He apologized for putting me to so much trouble.

So this evening I put on my shantung dress, and at a quarter to seven I was shown straight into the office of Monsieur Grouillot, who rushed to greet me with the greatest—I almost said grossest—display of good will.

He's enormous, and looks all the more so because he isn't tall. When he totters about on his tiny little feet he looks as if he's about to keel over in one direction or another—I almost shoved away the mass of flesh that seemed to be toppling towards me.

But his sharp mobile glance reveals an intelligence that's also reflected in his conversation, which is sometimes flowery and sometimes rather vulgar, but never colorless. He couldn't have

got to the position he's in if he didn't possess remarkable qualities.

He said at once, "I am very happy, mademoiselle, to kiss the
charming hand that's so well disposed towards me and has already done me such unforgettable service in so few words."

Straightening up again, he added mischievously, "You have a
surprisingly concise style!"

The ice had been skillfully broken.

He then showed me around his establishment. The staff was
just packing up to go home, but he included every department,
accompanying the tour of inspection with a mass of information—often either confidential or jesting—about the efficiency
of the organization. I must say it was very interesting and quite
impressive. Especially the computer in the basement, which,
among other things, gives up-to-the-minute data on the state of
all stock.

Then we got into the back of a big midnight-blue car—just
to go a few hundred yards.

"We're going to have dinner in a private room at
Topolinski's," he informed me. "I'm quite old enough to take
you to a place like that, and in any case, virtue and respect-
ability are written all over you. As you may imagine, we've got
to have a serious talk—and as privately as possible."

What he referred to as Topolinski's was the renowned Lapérouse restaurant on the boulevard des Grands-Augustins. The
rococo private rooms there are certainly charming, and the special dishes are served with sauces nothing short of sublime. But
there was a melon that left something to be desired, on the
subject of which my host first apologized to me at great length
and then made some sour remarks to the headwaiter. I felt
quite sorry for him. I never like to complain, myself.

But to come to the point . . .

Grouillot began by asking me how I found out about the plagiarism. Then he wanted to know how many copies of the two
volumes there might still be in the "Amsterdam edition, at the
Company's expense," or any reprint at the Bibliothèque nationale or elsewhere. He seemed overjoyed at my rough guess,
which was that most of them must have found their way long
ago to the United States, the museum of Europe. And he was

also delighted to hear that despite the recent revival in Prévost studies, researchers usually confine themselves to his best-known work.

Grouillot then cleared his throat and delivered an elegant speech.

"Mademoiselle, the inquiries I immediately instituted about you—I apologize now that I know you better, but put yourself in my place!—show you to be a pious young lady, attentive to all your duties. So you will understand when I say that I, who am already getting on in years and by the nature of things am obliged to live in a very impure world, seek from you, in your enlightened innocence, advice in an unprecedented situation which is first and foremost a matter of ethics.

"I am in a position of the most painful perplexity.

"It would certainly be very unpleasant for me to let this plagiarism continue. The public has been just as taken in as I was. But if you think about it carefully, they haven't been deceived by the quality of the goods so much as by the label, and even that in a favorable sense, in so far as an exceptional product is being sold under an ordinary ticket. What I am really doing is providing people with salmon in sardine tins.

"I joke in order to amuse you, but there's some truth in what I say! And remember that without the subterfuge, which with good reason is troubling us, this undoubted masterpiece wouldn't be available for sale at all. You saw that the paperback edition of the *Grecque moderne* was only a partial success. To print more than a hundred thousand of a Prévost rescued from oblivion, there had to be special circumstances, circumstances which could converge only in my establishment, and from which, in the last analysis, the public has profited most. In short, it was that or nothing! And the marvelous text from the 'Amsterdam edition, at the Company's expense,' which is bringing cultural enrichment into a hundred thousand homes—isn't that much better than nothing?"

As a result of these entertaining attempts to convince me, the generous amounts of nectar I'd been fed, and the piquancy of the last remark, which was not lost on me, I burst out laughing. And since this seemed to take Grouillot aback, I explained that I thought it showed a certain amount of humor, saddling him with a plagiarism "at the Company's expense."

He agreed, but then grew serious again and handed me a letter, which I read to the accompaniment of his comments.

"No, the scoundrel certainly isn't lacking in humor, and still less in cynicism. He doesn't feel the slightest remorse. Just look at this billet-doux, the first he's sent me since he got one foot out of the grave. Look, the blackest ingratitude and venality flaunting themselves in letters of gold. He tells me off for not selling his black sheep for a high enough price! In all my experience with swindlers I've never seen such a thing. And I got it by the very same mail delivery that brought me your own kind letter. Just think of me sitting there with one in each hand! I nearly had apoplexy."

I'd become serious myself on seeing the handwriting of one whom for a time I'd been blind enough to call "Dominique." What cynicism, yes, what baseness! Yet again I couldn't believe my eyes.

Grouillot, who'd gone brick red at the thoughts he'd just been conjuring up, then went on more calmly.

"You can imagine, mademoiselle, how glad I'd be to see this devious, impudent wretch end up in a cell on wet straw—he must have done the whole thing more to harm me than to further his own reputation.

"I never could stand the sight of him. Like you, I'm of the people. I was born in a little town in Corrèze, not far from Bourbonnais, the region of your own almost equally humble origins. Labattut-Largaud has all the bourgeois intellectual's contempt, whether open or concealed, for those who've had to pull themselves up by their own bootlaces, without a solid backing or a brilliant university career. It would be a pure serene joy for me to get the wretch locked up.

"But unfortunately prisons aren't what they used to be in my young days. Once he was inside, Béba Vesport would set to and plagiarize everything he could lay his hands on, and be better off than ever!

"Above all, what would be the result for masses of innocent people?

"My own life's work would be turned to ridicule, the international image I worked so hard to create would be destroyed forever.

"But never mind about me, suddenly exposed to the gibes and malice of my chief rivals. I'm getting on in years—sooner or later I'll have to forget about this Vanity Fair.

"But what about all the young people, all the deserving workers whose just claims I supported in May 1968, whose hopes I have never ceased to share and encourage, and who have always trusted me—do you think, in the present state of affairs, they'd be able to find other jobs if my firm collapsed?

"But I can't stop the locomotive now without making the boiler explode. A scandal of the first order! If I'd been lucky enough to discover the deception in time I wouldn't have hesitated to act: a prompt, energetic reaction would have minimized a certain inevitable amount of ridicule. But now it's too late . . . or too soon . . . A few years from now a scandal would do me far less harm—by then I'd share my own initial blindness with that of the whole world, which would forgive me in order to forgive itself. But now is the most difficult and vulnerable period there could possibly be for me . . .

"Help me, I beg you! Be kind! It's not only my reputation that's in your hands but that of a whole business which is a model of its kind, one great big family . . ."

By this time I was quite moved.

"What will you do with the money?" I asked.

"What money?"

"The money the book will make, of course—the money it's already making."

"I don't quite follow . . . What do you expect me to do with it but reinvest it? That's the law of the Medes and the Persians in business."

"I'm not an idiot—I mean your own personal profit, of course."

"But, mademoiselle, a French firm doesn't make any profit! I never have made any profit and never will. I don't know what it is and I don't want to know! Touch wood!"

"Are you making fun of me?"

"In my position it's the last thing I'd want. You don't understand because you don't know the setup. I'll be completely frank with you. Grouillot and Co. pays me a meager salary of nine thousand, nine hundred and seventy-one francs a month as Managing Director, plus twenty-four thousand francs expenses, out of which, if you'll forgive me for mentioning it, we are dining this evening. You can't yet be set against special expenses! I also get something for attending directors' meetings, a Company car, and a Company flat on the top floor of the building. I also put my business trips and all too rare vacations down to overhead. I don't mention dividends on the Company's shares, of which I hold fifty-one percent and which have been quoted on the Stock Exchange for seven years. Where's the profit in all that? Especially 'personal profit'? Horrible word! Now do you see how it works?"

"Very well."

"Good!"

"By reinvesting on the one hand and pushing up the expenses on the other, you end up with nothing from the tax point of view."

"Less than nothing! Like everyone else. And we have a devil of a time surviving under these conditions. But you talk as if this were General Motors!"

"Never mind about reinvestment—that has to do with the firm. But you yourself admit that your own personal profits come under overhead, which is artificially inflated. So it's easy to calculate how much it could be further inflated by the proceeds of the fraud, so that the money could go to charity."

Grouillot fished out a large handkerchief, mopped his brow, and contemplated me uneasily.

I pointed out that if, thanks to me, he held onto the proceeds of embezzlement, I would be his accomplice. And that could not be.

After a meditative silence Grouillot concluded that I must have some sordid ulterior motive. This led him to a yet more regrettable utterance.

"I think I see what you're getting at. So I'll put something aside for your works of charity. We'll perform prodigies of accountancy for them! But I advise you to open an account in Geneva just the same. It would be wiser. For both of us . . ."

I was so surprised, so hurt, so overwhelmed, that I left my soufflé. I just got up and walked out.

I looked so upset that as I was going down the stairs the white-haired headwaiter asked me if I was ill. I must have stammered out that Monsieur Grouillot had just behaved very badly. The man looked very sympathetic, and tried to make me stay and calm down.

And then Grouillot, who'd been lumbering down the stairs after me and must have witnessed the scene, burst out with the utmost coarseness against the poor headwaiter, who had been so kind.

"It's not what you think at all, you fathead! Why don't you look after your melons?"

That really was the last straw! Without waiting for explanations I rushed out in search of less polluted air.

Grouillot panted after me to the boulevard Saint-Michel, repeating over and over again that there'd been a misunderstanding.

In the end I turned around and said, "There has been no misunderstanding. I understood your dishonest proposition perfectly well. I no longer trust you, and can have no more to do with you."

He stood there looking after me in immense astonishment, mingled perhaps with a tinge of respect. It is possible that Monsieur Grouillot is not basically dishonest, like LL. I'll pray for him at mass on Sunday. He's on a downhill course.

Two in the morning already!

Anyhow, my duty is clear . . .

7/21/73

At this time of the morning I used to be still at "Dominique's" lectures.

I ought to write to him. I must. But I don't want to.

Buck up, Cécile! Putting it off won't help.

From the Private File of Labattut-Largaud

Tuesday
July 24, 1973

I've just been down to the café across the street and had a nice glass of mineral water for breakfast. As I crossed the road I was quite "intoxicated" by the air, to use Casanova's expression. He didn't always make the past participle agree with the subject, but he always made what he meant perfectly clear. He knew the only rule that matters is to give pleasure.

Coming up again in the elevator, I was imprisoned with Claire's fleeting lover. (The ambiguities of most languages! German is much clearer. One of these days I'll wreak absolute havoc plagiarizing *Faust!*)

The young man's handlebar moustache is getting scraggly and losing its architectural form. Soon it won't be able to tickle much of anything.

On the way up Whatever-his-name-is spoke to me for the first time in ages. Some commonplace remark about my health. And then he added, the idiot, as if I might suspect him of coming to see Claire, "I'm going up to see my fiancée on the fifth floor."

I congratulated him and said, "It's time you settled down!"

"I don't ask anything better," he said with a wry smile. "It's my fiancée who doesn't want to settle down!"

Ours is not an age in which marriage is taken seriously.

Friendly phone call from Grouillot. He apologized for having let the film rights go for next to nothing, and dangled various magnificent prospects before me.

"My desk is covered with interesting offers, my dear fellow. The United States, England, Germany, and Italy are all competing for the translation rights. But there's no hurry. Time is

97

on our side. I'll put *Equivocations* up for offers at the Frankfurt Book Fair. It opens at the beginning of October. Then you'll see some fireworks!"

Maybe. All that wheeling and dealing, at Frankfurt and everywhere else, leaves me cold. I've never been less interested in money. Do you think about cash when you're up to the neck in nitroglycerin?

10 P.M.

Received the following note at midday.

Cécile Dubois to Dominique Labattut-Largaud

Sir:

As Félix Grouillot does not seem inclined to put an end to the equivocations, I shall inform *Le Monde* towards the middle of August of that which out of respect for the public and myself I can no longer conceal. I have delayed too long already.

This warning will, I presume, enable you to put your affairs in order, and the time I have chosen, in the middle of the summer vacation, will do as much as possible to lessen the effect of a scandal, which I bitterly deplore.

You must face up to your responsibilities with as much courage as I do in writing these lines.

I shall always remember your kindness with pleasure.

Cécile Dubois

My intuition expected it so clearly that my reason was not unduly surprised. The trap is closing around me. But not quite. It could be worse. Let me think . . .

Grouillot has kept quiet. And he'll go on doing so. He'll wait it out while Cécile does her tricks, since he couldn't buy her. For if I know him, he tried. As if you could buy children! You can punish them, you can persuade them, you can deceive them. But they haven't got a price. Fool of a man! He must be going through it too. The thought almost consoles me.

And the form of the warning does leave some room for hope. The executioner's hand trembles. The procrastination. The mistakes. That she's waiting until the middle of August shows the young woman is badly upset. Cécile is condemning me and crying for help at the same time. With a bit of luck I may be able to put her off.

But why does she have to interfere? Is it for children to execute justice? You may say they're the only ones who can. But they always do it wrong. When all's said and done, I haven't deserved this!

One thing especially is encouraging. Judging by appearances and by the picture Grouillot is bound to have painted of me, she must take me to be a scoundrel of the worst kind. Whereas in fact it's just one of those unforeseen accidents, or rather several of them, as accidents never happen singly. Because of a virus, a practical joke which I would have nipped in the bud has got the bit between its teeth and become pseudonymous fame. It's a piece of extraordinary bad luck. It's not a disgrace.

If only I could manage to explain! But how? I haven't got the slightest proof that I acted in good faith. Anything I said would be so true it would sound horribly false!

Midnight

The only proof is my notebooks.

Very difficult. Very unpleasant. But if I hurry—so as to eliminate any suspicion of my having altered them retrospectively—their authenticity is indisputable. If I let Cécile read a few chosen extracts, surely she'd . . . But she wouldn't have to read one line too many! The way the plagiarism came into being, and my first reactions, ought to satisfy her.

But while I'm at it, wouldn't it be a good idea to alter them a bit? If I used a space here and there to add a few kind or even tender remarks, that would give the reader great pleasure. One little touch can turn friendship into . . . The stakes are so high!

I have to think of myself. I have to think of Claire and the children.

If I'm nabbed now, my name will be officially mud—and I'm not going to submit my notebooks to the tender mercies of the public in order to clear myself. If I did, my situation would be desperate, dishonorable, and irremediable. Claire would despise me, François and Chantal would laugh me to scorn, Toby would lift up his leg against me.

Claire, Chantal, and Toby—I could take that. But François? No, it would be unbearable.

François is worth a small impropriety.

I'll sleep on it. Have nightmares, rather.

From the Diary of Mademoiselle Cécile Dubois

7/26/73

Oh, I'm so happy! I knew the truth of the heart couldn't lie and that there are certain grave accents which cannot deceive! Rousseau said so, and religion before him. I knew deep down inside that Dominique's crime didn't exist because it couldn't exist, and that all the so-called evidence was not enough to prove it or even suggest it. And I was right. No evidence can prove anything against feeling. And yesterday evening I had dazzling written proof of it!

At a quarter to nine there was a ring at the door. I'd already taken my slacks off. So I put on my dressing gown and went to the door. And what did I see in the half-light of the corridor? How can I express it? The Ghost from *Hamlet?* I recognized Dominique by his cane. Goodness, how changed he looked! All thin and scraggly and still a bit yellow. Quite pitiful.

The unfortunate creature, leaning on his cane, tottered over to poor Mama's chair and collapsed into it. It's a bit too small for him.

He had a sky-blue folder under his arm, and as he began to get his breath back he said:

"Exhausted! No taxis at La Muette. Phone out of order. Strikes on the subway. Buses full to bursting. Came on François's bike. Skidded on the Pont-Neuf. And to end up with, the stairs! Anyway, here I am. Very glad to see you again. Feel better already.

"Come and sit over here, my dear. I've brought you something to read. You seem to be interested in a case of plagiarism."

He opened his folder, which was full of rather grubby handwritten sheets of paper. I went over, understandably curious, while Dominique went through his notes, arranging them for me.

"You are the first person to look, with I hope an indulgent eye, on these notebooks. I keep them up year in year out, like Frédéric Amiel. They spend most of the time in my safe, and they will die with me.

"I didn't write them especially to deceive you—that would have been rather difficult in twenty-four hours! You can trust them.

"Go on, read them. They'll tell you more than any long speeches about a misunderstanding which led you astray for a while. Also about me, and about the unspeakable Grouillot, and the incredible bad luck I've had. I'm much more to be pitied than blamed!"

I sat down and leaned over and started to read the passages he pointed out to me with his diaphanous fingers. Overwhelmed with surprise and relief, I gradually realized how the temptation came to him, and what he had good reason to suppose would come of it: his freedom of expression destroyed by a cruel and unscrupulous businessman.

Every so often he would cover a passage with his hand, saying with a gentle smile which belied his words, "You mustn't look at that bit. I mention you too often. And it's not all praise. You have some little faults!"

But as he was commenting at some length on the chronological account of his agonizing rise to success, he was too late in covering up the bottom of one page. So I saw: "In my present plight my thoughts naturally turn to Cécile and the pleasant memories . . ." I don't dare remember the rest.

So Dominique, like me, had his secret: the delightful anxiety of "friendship that is something more than friendship." He looked humbly for the "verdict in [my] eyes, so severe and yet sometimes so gentle," and I might have driven him to suicide! What a lesson! That's what bold and hasty judgments lead to, which scorn the wisdom of instinct! I had tears in my eyes at the thought as Dominique went on:

"This page is dirty. A fishmonger's truck went over Lamartine after I fell off the bike on the Pont-Neuf. My wife and her lover, a couple of pages before, nearly fell into the Seine!"

Dear Dominique looked back on this possibility with a noble bitterness. It was a great proof of confidence on his part not to conceal from me certain of his disillusions. What sort of a woman would you have to be to deceive such a sensitive man?

He gathered the pages together and shut the folder.

I thought it appropriate to deliver a little sermon.

"You see where imprudence and dubious contrivance get you. Not all means are justified, even in pursuit of an honorable end. You wanted to make use of Prévost to get back your freedom and dignity, but he, by a fortunate counterstroke, caught you in the snare of a fame that belongs in the first place to him. Let that be a warning to you!"

Dominique groaned. "It's a warning, all right!"

But I could see that my unspoken indulgence was reviving him.

"That's all very well," I said, "but what about the money? What are you going to do with that?"

"What money?"

"The money the book will make, of course—the money it's making already."

"I don't quite follow . . . What do you expect me to do with it? It's mine—I stole it."

Fortunately I soon saw he was joking—a good sign, given the terrible state he was in when he came.

I suggested he should devote all the proceeds of the deception to charity. But human weakness is such even in the best of men that he wasn't very keen. The prospect of peace and quiet, uncertain and temporary as it was, seemed to revive his interest in Mammon and his works.

Thinking he might be persuaded to act from self-serving motives, I said:

"Your sentence is only suspended. Sooner or later the scandal may come out. And then the complete sacrifice I advise you to make would be the only thing that would ensure you a favorable press. Grouillot won't do any such thing. Think it over!"

He seemed extremely struck and interested by this thought. Whatever anyone may say, the end does sometimes justify the means!

We spoke some more about Grouillot, and I had to tell all the details of the dinner in the private room at Lapérouse. Including my hasty departure.

"Has it occurred to you," asked Dominique, "that Grouillot gets even more than I do out of this? And that you were refusing a fortune? You're a saint!"

Then I said, rather vexed at being so little understood:

"When we do our duty we are only good servants doing our work. There is nothing for us to boast about. Saintliness consists in doing more than that. And saints don't boast because they are saints."

At that he patted me gently on the knee and said:

"Don't you boast, then. Let me do the praising. I enjoy it so much!"

It was the first time Dominique's hand had touched any other part of me except my own hand. At once, in spite of myself, I felt greatly stirred, and this immediately put me right on my guard against all the imprudences I must not indulge in. I lowered my eyes, and by a lucky chance saw Gustave sharpening his claws on Dominique's stripped trousers. This down-to-earth incident brought me to my senses, and I took advantage of it to put a stop to the conversation.

I can only be a good influence on Dominique if I avoid even the appearance of dangerous tenderness. I must not encourage either his weakness or my own. The heart can fall into traps, just as plagiarism can.

My greatest happiness is not to be placed in vain hopes. It is that I have had restored to me a real friend who needs help and good advice.

As he was leaving Dominique suddenly asked:

"Tell me, how did you find out?"

I kept him just long enough to tell him about the link between Prévost and Aïssé, which led straight to the truth and the solution of the anagram.

No doubt with a touch of flattery, Dominique professed to be taken aback by my perspicacity. I remember him exclaiming, "It's a good thing there aren't two like you!"

But I thought he seemed slightly vexed at having sinned through ignorance of a detail of literary history after having put so much erudition into his work. He won't boast about that! Whom could he boast to, anyway?

He's going to La Claustraies on August 1 to finish convalescing. So I shan't see him for a whole month.

Dear Dominique!

From the Private File of Labattut-Largaud

Thursday
July 26, 1973

Good God! That was a close one! I'll have been saved from pastiche and plagiarism by falsity! Sympathetic homeopathy! I feel almost myself again.

Cécile is a treasure. Not only will she keep quiet, like Grouillot, but her idea of giving the money away is positively inspired. Simple people often see things more clearly than clever ones. If I carry out meticulously the plan of giving the money to charity, I can be sure of what matters most—moral and psychological tranquillity. If I'm caught red-handed but my hand is empty, I can look the public and my children in the face. And the indignation of the righteous will concentrate by contrast on that Shylock of a Grouillot, who wouldn't give a sinking Ophelia a glass of water. I'm reviving!

By a crowning touch of thoughtfulness Cécile has discreetly put Grouillot in the picture, which removes a terrible threat that would otherwise have hung over me. Now he and I are both party to a secret in which that crook has an even greater interest than I have, if possible. And I have the delightful bonus of watching Grouillot's anguish as he cooks up all future contracts—on the edge of a volcano, expecting his inkwell to be submerged by lava at any moment!

What a saint of a girl! I'm ready to kiss her hands, her eyes, any part of her, like a relic! I'll send the tomcat in heat who pees on my pants a can of sardines and a fancy can opener! I'm resuscitating!

Now I'm feeling better, I'll play a trick on Grouillot, who's concealed his interview with Cécile for reasons that can only be unworthy. Or perhaps simply because he's afraid of appearing even more ridiculous.

I shall take the opportunity to win myself a good press by piously hiving off the loot to charity. It must be done now. If I leave it till tomorrow I might leave it altogether.

So let's say something like this:

> Dear Friend:
> This (registered) letter is to request you to pay into the post office account of the Orphans of Auteuil all future royalties due to me from any source now or in the future for the novel *Equivocations*. By the same post I am myself sending to the protégés of little Saint Thérèse of Lisieux the moneys I have already received for the book.
> Such a decision is in the great traditions of the University of France, to which I have the honor to belong. A pastiche so perfect that it takes its place effortlessly among the classics that crown our culture should not bring its author any personal gain. It should at once be made to benefit the whole community, and in particular the underprivileged.
> May the Spirit of the University inspire you with

similar disinterestedness! Your whole past career cries out to me that you will not be deaf to this suggestion.

Yours, etc.

Grouillot is legally obliged to preserve in his archives the original of every order of this kind.

He can make himself paper airplane out of the postscript:

P.S. I am happy to tell you that with a few lines I have obtained for us the good will of Mlle D.

All the effect of my own style upon a noble spirit was needed to counteract the deplorable impression you managed to make in a few hours upon this irreproachable young woman, who is also one of my most assiduous students.

I could see she was still overwhelmed by the odious proposition that after much laborious maneuvering you had the audacity to make to her. She told me the details with all the innocence of a child.

But what her outraged modesty would have blushed to reveal I learned by chance yesterday evening at T.'s, where I went to sustain life on a Cavaillon melon and an undressed salad: there I learned of your wretched attempt at libertinism in a private room, from which your victim could escape only by headlong flight. The old headwaiter—and Heaven knows he's had plenty of experience!—was still in a state of shock.

Corrupting the mind isn't enough for you. Unable to aspire higher after all your excesses, you wanted to leave your slimy trail on the one path in the last virgin forest where unsullied virtue might find refuge!

What sort of man are you, my poor Félix? I knew you were a bit of a rogue and inclined to obscenity, but I did think you were a better diplomat than that!

A good thing I was at hand to inspire confidence!

That'll please him again. His kind are particularly furious at being accused of something they didn't do.

Claire, who's been trying to make up her mind what color

mink she likes best, will also be furious at my grandiose generosity. Pleasant scenes in prospect! A bit of an effort in bed when I'm strong enough won't take the place of a fur coat. But it's the lesser of two evils.

Sunday
July 29, 1973

Nearly every evening Mlle Dubois ruins my Spartan gruel by a phone call about my health and my appetite. She is now as knowledgeable on the subject of hepatitis as on that of plagiarism, and can go on for ten minutes about the CR 326 virus that one Hilleman has recently isolated in silky marmosets. I know I wrote somewhere that I'd like to hear her wise voice again. But this is too much. I'd never have dreamed she was such a jabbermouth. Hurry vacation and La Claustraies—where I've been waiting seven years to get a telephone!

That young woman's affections seem to be just waiting to smother someone. It's understandable. She's absolutely exhausted by virtue. She's been living by herself ever since her paralytic Mama has no longer been there to bring a spark of life into the place. She's bored. And even Gustave can't satisfy her longing for a higher friendship. He's too wholly engrossed in himself.

It is only friendship she feels for me. But is that quite certain?

I see it's a crucial question. Even Cécile's friendship is no laughing matter. If she loves me I may as well make my will straightaway.

But let us examine the matter closely. I'm nearly twice as old as she is. I'm not especially good-looking or attractive. I'm too interested in myself to interest women, whose first requirement is that one should think about them. I'm a married man and a deceived husband (rather less than most, but it's a fact). There's nothing in all that to turn the head of a pious young woman, balanced, sensible, quite pretty, with her life before her, either in the fulfillment of a suitable marriage or in the demanding vocation of celibacy. Right, then.

No more arguments, since love is a shameful disease of reason. If Cécile had been foolish enough to be in love with me, I would have had enough opportunity to notice it. But however thoroughly I search my memory, I can't find the slightest sign. And love is something which throws the usual mechanisms out of order and is bound to be noticed sooner or later. But even the telephone calls are poles apart from coquetry or the slightest eroticism—they're just boring.

To put it at its worst, Cécile might feel for me "a friendship that is something more than friendship," as I've written somewhere. But you can't make a consuming passion out of 3 percent of latent sexuality. The same interest rate as the post office.

Moreover, she's clearly a cold-blooded animal. It's a proven fact that saints don't have the same organs as everyone else. It's a species that rarely reproduces, and then in the manner of fish. Which is why the early Christians made the fish the symbol of the long-range love they bore one another.

Buffon writes somewhere to Mlle de Lespinasse: "If one is to believe Pliny the Elder, who may have come upon some of them in the vivarium at Pompeii, the male saint, fluttering about with compunction in propitious semidarkness, sanctimoniously deposits his milt on the string of translucent eggs that the female saint, on nights of full moon, leaves at the entrance to some cave. So careful is the male saint, so absentminded is the female . . ."* This way of going on is very heartening.

According to some authors, the female saint, properly speaking, has more warmth. But did not the Oratorian Malebranche, whose bitch was famous for her lack of amorousness, tell Newton in the course (probably) of a hunting party, "A female saint is like my bitch—unconscious both of the knocks I give and the kicks I feel."*

No, I can sleep easily. Friendship is quite enough for me. Especially as, in the situation I've got myself into, the wishes of Cécile are my commands. I must just trust to her natural discretion, which unfortunately is not as great as might be wished.

* Editor's note: Long and patient research has virtually established that these passages are not by Buffon or Malebranche.

I have the disagreeable impression that all the feelings of whatever kind I might have had for Cécile have been poisoned and reduced to nothing by the threat she has made me live under, in some form or another, ever since she started to take notice of me. And it's getting worse—my smiles have never been so forced.

Monday
July 30, 1973

Drove in a taxi this afternoon through gradually emptying Paris to rue Monsieur-le-Prince and back. Edelberger, the Assistant Director, had begged me to call before I leave for La Claustraies in order to sign two hundred copies with the name "Béba Vesport" for the benefit of deserving booksellers. It was Grouillot's idea, but I could scarcely refuse.

After one's been ill or away it's always with a tinge of emotion that one sees again the heart of Paris and the unassuming river that makes it beat. The setting is on a human scale, charged with a history most people no longer understand—all they remember is a few caricatures. And is not history, interpreted by ushers, much more the opium of the people than religion? Left-wing history and right-wing history are as good one as the other when it comes to fools' paradises.

I was in Edelberger's office, signing, and he'd gone out for a minute when Grouillot burst in and nearly fell over me. I had my back to him. I automatically got up.

"Oh, it's you!" said Grouillot, his face suddenly distorted with hatred and aversion. "You again!"

"More than ever," I answered jovially. "From now on I'm a column of the Temple, a pillar of the House!"

This nearly made Grouillot lose control of himself.

"A putrefying pillar," he spat out under his breath.

". . . in Ali Baba's cave," I replied out of the corner of my mouth.

We set about getting it off our chests, with Grouillot continuing to insult me.

"Vile plagiarist!"

"Mere accomplice!"

"Unmitigated scoundrel!"

"Fat moron!"

"Conceited ass!"

"Donkey-eared swindler!"

"Parchment villain!"

"Gaullist!"

"Oh, that's too much!"

I shall never know to what extremes the crescendo would have taken Grouillot, for at that moment the stargazing Edelberger, followed by the guileless Mme Fenouille, came back into his office, and Grouillot, afraid they might have overheard one word too many, tried to pull the wool over their eyes by falling into my arms and kissing and cuddling and fawning over me.

What a delicious moment! A consolation in itself for I don't know how many things.

I've booked a table at the Tour d'Argent tomorrow evening for Cécile and myself. I owe her one last attention before La Claustraies. It may as well be such as to flatter her a bit. And I shan't mind having a chance to sniff out if there are any whiffs of love about her. However hard I try to drive out the suspicion, it still bothers me.

And Cécile is now one of those who are in charge of the Prévost collection, where my two volumes sleep with one eye open. That's food for thought.

A garage mechanic who's a collector has found a period gasket for my car. So on the morning of August 1, despite the sarcastic remarks of my madly modern children, I shall be able to drive off with my mind at rest.

Tuesday
July 31, 1973

A messenger from Grouillot's came early this morning with an unsigned letter typed on a discreet portable and not on the official IBM machine with a ball. That really is a laugh!

But what it says is very interesting.

Because of the rather excited words we exchanged with equal mutual esteem, I prefer not to speak to you personally of what I have in mind. I have to be careful of my heart.

But I can tell you your instructions about the payments will be scrupulously carried out.

I had thought the matter over urgently on my own account, and come to the same conclusions as those you arrived at somewhat late in the day. As early as it was feasible on the morning after my dinner at T.'s, I made the necessary arrangements for the benefit of the children's holiday camps run by the Socialist party. We shall thus be covered from both sides.

I congratulate you unreservedly on ensuring the good will of Mlle D. In the circumstances it seems to me that the following suggestion is a reasonable one: in September, by a few carefully calculated indiscretions, the mask of the pseudonym might be removed. There is less and less reason for it, and indeed, kept up permanently, it might prove to be a nuisance.

However striking they may be for a time, successes due to curiosity soon begin to flag. Setting up your real image in all its grandeur, to the accompaniment of suitable publicity, would give the whole thing a fresh impetus.

From the financial point of view, such a revival of interest in you and all your possibilities would in the first place bring many advantages to the charities we both have so much at heart. A second advantage would be that it might at last be possible to make some profit from the judicious publishing of historical novels. This honorable and highly salable kind of book, written with the particular verve you are sometimes capable of, and presented under a well-known name, seems to me to offer possibilities which should not be neglected. Given the extent of your generosity, that's the only way we can make any money.

But there is also the question of security.

If you acknowledged E. as yours, we could put your imperishable masterpiece up for an important literary prize when the new season begins in October. A success of this kind—and to its promotion I would devote every effort I am still capable of, despite "all [my] excesses"—would be an immense help to us in case of accident, which is always possible. In such an event it would not be a bad thing to have taken the precaution of associating with our huge success a dozen or so clear-sighted and influential pundits, who could set about pouring oil and balm into the workings of the press. I am thinking of the Prix F., the jury of which includes many more than the average number of members of the French Academy and of the Académie Gon-court.

Similarly, the abandoning of the pseudonym could only help in the auction I propose to hold at the coming Book Fair in Frankfurt. It would be an excellent thing if we could sell the translation rights of E. to foreign publishers of international importance.

In short, what I recommend is a sort of forward retreat. But to retreat in that direction is, paradoxically enough, the wisest thing to do, for in that way we expand our circle into one big family which will have the same interest as we do in maintaining your reputation and my own.

I will not expatiate on the fact that by following my advice you will be able for once in your life to enjoy all the heady fumes of fame and pride that your original talents can satisfy in no other way.

To encourage you to join me in this policy, I am holding at your disposal an advance of 50,000 francs. Until something more comes in to tide you over, that should be enough to enable you to butter up the skinny slut who shares your yoke and whom the ground-floor bull used formerly to cover when he pleased, while you were both already conjugally lowering your horned heads towards my trough.

I should be obliged if you would let me have your answer before you leave tomorrow. The matter is urgent: a campaign of this kind takes time to organize. You know my home telephone number if the office should be closed. I shall be glad to hear you say "Cuckoo" again.

P.S. Mlle D. will tell you the honest truth about my virtue, should you care to inquire. She cannot lie: she is too good for this world.

Her kind discretion over E. does not surprise me. Women who are real Christians have even more kindness than righteousness, which fortunately means that what they do has no effect on events. Furthermore, I myself offered some pretty forceful arguments which no doubt have sunk in.

When I left her I would have been prepared to bet that in spite of everything her behavior would come up to scratch. And every day since that has passed without a scandal has proved the correctness of my diagnosis.

But be very careful. Mlle D. has to be managed by means of the Bible. I was foolish enough to strike a false note. Make sure you don't do the same!

Will Claire have her mink for the autumn, then?

The dirty swine! Grouillot's just the sort to institute systematic private investigations about anyone who's unwise enough to have anything to do with him! What a sly trick—just like him! He soils everything he touches. I expect his files and card indexes are full of information with which he could sully the reputation of anyone in Paris who's still considered respectable. Even the Bible is only an instrument to him! Nothing is sacred!

But you can't say he doesn't understand business. As he says, to remove the mask would make things easier for me all around. I've often noticed one always ends up by coming to terms with nimble-witted rogues. In life it's the fools who are the most dangerous.

The idea of picking up the Prix Fénelon is very attractive. It doesn't usually mean particularly large sales, but it's true that all those august academic presences make up for that. If I can make eminent French Academicians give a prize to Prévost by means of my humble self, then if anything goes wrong green uniforms will spring up on all sides and struggle frantically with swords and cocked hats to slay the dragon. If I weren't me, how I'd split my sides!

"Forward retreat"—an apt phrase.

It's time for me to finish packing and get dressed to climb the Tour d'Argent.

The dinner with my tyrannical chartist was on the whole a success, apart from some slight agitation towards the end.

So as to salve my conscience and not to have to worry about her really caring for me, I set her quite a subtle trap, about which I'm quite pleased with myself. It was inspired by Claire's former unfaithfulness. And later on, by chance, I was given another definitive proof.

Cécile doesn't love me from afar, nor near to, nor very near to. And if she doesn't love me already, it's hard to see why she ever should. Phew, what a relief!

At about midnight I phoned Grouillot from the Tour d'Argent. I woke him up and said, "Cuckoo!" And he said, in the words of De Gaulle, "I have understood." And then we both hung up. A triumph of taciturnity.

Cécile "staggers" her holidays, and takes a fortnight at the end of August and a fortnight at Christmas. She spends both fortnights in the Bourbonnais, staying with a surviving aunt.

Meanwhile she has promised to put my two volumes out of harm's way for some little time to come. This favor alone would have been enough to make the dinner a success.

Seeing how long I shall be away, I was tempted to take my notebooks with me to La Claustraies, but there's no safe there and accidents easily happen.

I'm tired out. Better go to bed, where I'll tell Claire that the concierge must have blabbed about her brief infidelity. It'll be a lesson to her, both in virtue and in discretion. Being betrayed like that is as bad as being betrayed twice!

From the Diary of
Mademoiselle Cécile Dubois

Sunday
8/5/73

Dominique loves me. And much more than I would ever have guessed!

I have been sure of it ever since Tuesday night's dinner at the Tour d'Argent, at which I was so preoccupied I can't even remember what I ate. Perhaps it was duck—I think it was served twice, in two different ways. But I remember Dominique had only a slice of Parma ham because of his diet. He'd only chosen the Tour for my sake. And I remember Notre-Dame all lit up—I could see it there below me all through the meal. Sometimes I looked at Dominique and sometimes I looked at Notre-Dame.

For five days now I've been going over and over in my mind what he said to me and what I said to him. And the more I think about it the surer I am that my first reaction was right. That was the only answer I could give.

Soon after the meal began, Dominique started to unburden himself more and more openly about his marital disillusionments. I was touched by his confiding in me, of course, but also very embarrassed. What is a girl to say when a gentleman of a certain age tells her his wife leaves something to be desired? I sympathized politely and tried to change the subject.

But Dominique kept on about his one idea, and before long he'd got to the point where he was talking about divorce and asking my opinion.

As it was difficult for me to put myself in his place and see into his personal problems, I thought the best thing to do was to treat the subject theoretically, so I naturally said I hadn't anything against divorce as such. This seemed to surprise him.

I briefly explained.

"The Church I belong to needs take no cognizance of divorce because it takes no cognizance of civil marriage. The Church concerns itself only with religious marriage and where necessary declares it null. This is quite a different thing from divorce. So you can ask for a divorce or a separation without actually going against the Gospels. What you can't do, if you wish to respect the Scriptures, is marry again while your partner is still living. If you did you would be committing adultery and bigamy in the sight of God.

"But you have been taught all that just the same as I have."

Dominique seemed puzzled.

"I thought," he said cautiously, "that the Gospels weren't very clear on the subject. Or at least that it was very much debated."

I simply quoted the words of Christ in Saint Mark: "'Whosoever shall put away his wife, and marry another, committeth adultery against her. And if a woman shall put away her husband, and be married to another, she committeth adultery.'"

Then I said, "With whom would you propose to debate that? Jesus Christ?"

Dominique sighed.

"You really are very severe! And that doesn't suit me at all. I don't mind confessing, seeing the friendliness of our relations, that the reason I toy with the idea of divorce is of course that I have secret hopes of marrying again before very long. I shall soon be forty-six. It's not too late to start a new life with some serious and educated young woman who's managed to make me trust her."

These last words were accompanied by a penetrating and significant look. I couldn't have been mistaken.

It suddenly seemed as if the huge dining room, with its crystal and its lights, were swaying to and fro; as if Notre-Dame had started to float away down the river. Dominique went on with what he was saying, but for a moment I didn't hear him.

Goodness, what a shock! Dominique loved me! It was quite a different thing from "the friendship that is something more than friendship." A man who was beyond reproach and had been deceived by an unworthy wife wanted quite naturally, almost morally, "to start a new life with some serious and educated young woman," one whose "gentle eyes" were there before him. Everything urged me to go along with him: reason itself, to a certain extent; the feelings which in spite of myself overwhelmed me; even the thought of the good I could do two poor children in danger of perdition from a broken home. What a terrible temptation! In a flash I had a vision of a whole life with my Dominique, years of mutual trust and confidence and esteem, the children we might have had. I even toyed with a fleeting thought inspired by quite permissible desire. And contemporary manners, what everyone else does, also made me indulge in that ostensibly honorable dream. I was weak enough to hesitate for a few seconds. If only Dominique hadn't made me sit facing Notre-Dame!

Anyhow, I pulled myself together in time! I returned to that higher love which should illumine all we do and which cannot admit of the least inconstancy.

I took refuge in a coldness I was very far from feeling, and pretended I hadn't heard.

But Dominique wouldn't let me off so lightly. Instead, mercilessly, he sought out the powerful arguments a cultivated lover knows how to find when he believes his fate depends upon his words.

"My dear Cécile, you're more royalist than the King! You know very well that nowadays devout divorcees who have married again while their first husband or wife is still alive are admitted to communion in your churches, with the encouragement of your bishops and the paternal tolerance of His Holiness. For all that Rome claims to maintain the indissolubility of marriage, it is even clearer that if she admits 'adulterers and bigamists' to the Eucharist, it's because adultery and bigamy are not what they were: they do not preclude moral improvement through contact with the Immaculate Host, nor even saintliness itself. Would you withhold from me the hope of one day becoming, in the company of some charming lady, the first adulterous and bigamous saint?

"Better still, if possible—your Church makes a great ceremony of blessing civil marriages which baptized Catholics have contracted without any immediate concern for sacramental and religious marriage. Forty cases of concubinage are to be blessed at Lugny, in the Mâconnais, on August 4—that is, in four days' time!

"Be logical, my dear Cécile! If my bigamy is Eucharistic, or if my concubinage is worthy of a blessing, why should you deny me them?

"You must see Rome implicitly admits that indissolubility is no longer anything but a myth or an unfortunate mistake. You must move with the times, and with your secular Church, which cannot err. How can you be so proud? Would you claim to know better than your archbishop and your Pope, who get such universally good press? For make no mistake: by forbidding me the remarriage I so fervently long for, you simply convict Rome of heresy. How frightful! And would you sacrifice me to such a whim?"

What could I answer? It was diabolical!

I decided to tell Dominique that nothing could do away with the Gospels. And I quoted Pascal: " 'Kings may give away their kingdoms, but popes may not give away theirs.' "

Dominique put on a scandalized expression. I finished him off with another quotation from the same author: " 'Even if my letters are condemned in Rome, what I condemn in them is condemned in heaven. I appeal to your judgment, Lord Jesus!' "

My poor Dominique fell silent. It was as heart-rending for him as it was for me. But he made a great effort to look calm, and so did I. We understood each other by hints.

For a while we talked about commonplace matters, and then Dominique brought the conversation around to the two Prévost volumes which were among those I was now in charge of. For the sake of peace and quiet I finally agreed to send them for repair, though only one of them really needed it. How weak I am! Anyway, at the rate that department works they'll be there for some time.

It was getting late when Dominique told me that Grouillot, in order to increase his profits, planned to abandon the pseudonym in September, to market *Equivocations* at the Frankfurt Book Fair, and to promote the book for the Prix Fénelon. Dominique was naturally vexed at having an usurped reputation thrust upon him like that. But what could he do, faced with a man like Grouillot?

I was startled to hear that the Marquis de la Pierre-Fondue, who is said to have written some very perspicacious things about Louis XV's favorites and the Chevalier d'Éon, was to be a member of the jury.

"Has it occurred to you," I asked Dominique, "that if the French Academy, in the person of the marquis, gives a prize to this disgraceful plagiarism, the whole illustrious body will be in danger of ridicule?"

Dominique gave a groan of anguish.

"That would be the worst possible punishment for my imprudence! Spare me, please! If only you knew . . ."

What can I myself do against a man like Dominique? And from now on I risk being an accomplice in this disgraceful affair simply by being silent. How one evil leads to another!

It was nearly midnight when we left. Before we did so, Dominique went into a phone booth. The door came open without his noticing as he picked up the receiver.

With a strangely mischievous air, considering the poignant sadness of the meal we'd just sat through, he said, "Cuckoo!" and hung up.

I don't think I've ever been so surprised in my life. Who on earth could he have been saying "Cuckoo!" to at that hour?

I felt an absurd qualm of jealousy. What woman of easy virtue was my Dominique going to meet in the middle of the night, after having unveiled his deepest feelings to me beside an illumined Notre-Dame? Was Dominique a cheat?

Or had I, blinded by my own feelings, been grossly mistaken about the identity of the "serious young woman" to whom Dominique wished to be united? Of course he hadn't been very explicit, although his way of going about it seemed to speak for itself.

But does one say "Cuckoo!" at midnight to a serious young woman? Had Dominique committed a new and fatal imprudence by seeking the hand of some frivolous female, as if his first mistake were not enough?

I didn't know where I was. But be that as it may, I was horribly disappointed at the thought that Dominique didn't love me, had never loved me, would never love me. When all the time I ought to have been thanking God on my knees—for both of us!

Out on the sidewalk by the river the doorman got us a taxi. Dominique could keep it after the short journey from there to the rue Saint-Jacques.

In the taxi Dominique, who seemed in excellent humor and somehow relieved, chattered away while I was sunk in a silence and agitation to which he paid no attention.

I couldn't resist asking, "Did you hear some good news on the telephone?"

"The best possible news!" he answered, as if it were possible for all his wishes to be fulfilled in two seconds. Then, noticing at last that I was on tenterhooks, he added, "I called up Gustave, to make sure he was really at home. He assures you of his fidelity."

Why didn't I leave it at that! But this answer put me beside myself, and I exclaimed, "So now you say 'Cuckoo!' to cats! How can you be so lacking in trust, Dominique? Aren't I your friend?"

Dominique was very crestfallen. Then, carried away by a very understandable bitterness, he said, "Curiosity will be the death of you, Cécile! You'd do better to think of all the unnecessary distress your damned inquisitiveness has caused me already! And you still go on with it this evening, which was supposed to have been a treat for both of us."

I had the unconscious cruelty to observe, "That doesn't answer my question."

"You absolutely insist on an explanation, then!" he cried in exasperation. "Let me tell you then, mademoiselle, that I was telephoning my wife to make sure she was in her own bed and not someone else's. And I said 'Cuckoo!' because 'Cuckoo!' is the cry of the cuckold. I didn't say anything else because it so happens I'm the only cuckold about at the moment, and that by itself was enough to identify me, and there are certain painful conversations which husbands prefer not to draw out, either with their faithless wives or with indiscreet young chartists. But, by heaven, you've sworn to make me drag out a living death in perpetual fear and humiliation!"

I burst into tears. It must have been so pitiful a sight that the too kind Dominique was upset himself. He patted me on the right thigh to console me. And as my sobs continued, he took me in his arms to pat me on the back in a chaste and friendly manner, like General Franco welcoming General de Gaulle when he was still in a position to be embraced.

I was overwhelmed. I no longer even realized the possible dangers of the situation, there in the dark in the back of a taxi, which had just double-parked outside where I live.

In such circumstances it was really too much to ask of the propriety of a man who though respectful was sincerely in love that he should remain as cold as marble very long. I felt a hand encircling my left breast and exerting gentle pressures. And Dominique was murmuring in my ear:

"All right, I forgive you. I'll put up with your being inquisitive if I must . . . because I'm very fond of you."

My prostration now gave way to waves of satisfaction in the depths of which I seemed to melt. I should have liked this, Dominique's first and last caress, to last a hundred years—like a first and last communion! I called on all the saints in heaven to save me, especially Saint Christopher, since we happened to be in a car. And at that moment the driver, who was beginning to get impatient, tapped on the bulletproof glass that separated him from us. The symbolism was striking.

Now it was my turn to murmur.

"I think you are forgetting yourself, Dominique!" I said.

And by another miracle he didn't wait to be told twice but apologized at once.

As I set myself to rights I assumed a severe look and said, "If you want to be the first adulterous and bigamous saint, at least wait until you're remarried! Until further orders the conciliar Church is very strict on that point!"

That struck home. But Dominique's way of expressing his sorrow was heart-rending.

"I shan't be like an old priest hearing confession and ask, 'Did you take pleasure in it, my child?' The answer I'd get is only too plain. I'm obviously not made to excite passion. Even friendship refuses me the most innocent favor in passing. In short, Gustave's the only one who gets excited about my trousers."

He opened the door of the taxi for me.

"Ah well, 'Cuckoo,' Cécile! Good-bye until September. Sweet dreams!"

I deceived him so easily!

I wept all night, and with good reason.

It's like something out of Racine.

From the Private File of
Labattut-Largaud

La Claustraies, Thursday
September 13, 1973

Received a letter from Mlle Dubois, which I'll put tomorrow among the notebooks awaiting me in the safe in the rue de la Pompe. But as nothing locks here and I'm well known for my absent-mindedness, I'll keep this development on me until our forthcoming departure. Prevention is better than cure!

> Mlle Cécile Dubois to Monsieur Dominique Labattut-Largaud
> La Claustraies
> Oise
>
> My dear Dominique:
> Your kind postcard reached me safely at the end of August at Bourbon-l'Archambault, with the better news of your health and your decision to stay longer than planned at La Claustraies in order to get entirely back to normal. You are quite right not to return until the fifteenth. Paris life and literary activity don't really begin again before the end of September.
> You will have been surprised by my long silence.

But the misunderstandings that marked our last meeting, and the liberties you permitted yourself in circumstances which didn't excuse everything, caused me to adopt a reserve which I am sure you'll understand. It does not affect the esteem and the warm friendship which I shall continue to feel for you. A sympathy such as that which exists between us is above any second aberration.

I stayed in Bourbon from August 15 to the thirty-first, and spent a very restful holiday of the kind which puts things in their proper place and enables one to face the future with suitable serenity.

The place is as delightful as ever, there beneath its ruined château. It is the former capital of the duchy, and usually a sleepy little town, but during the holidays there is a certain amount of stir, partly because of the baths, which in olden times were much frequented. Bourbon-l'Archambault was already fashionable at the time of Louis XIV, even more so than nowadays.

I went for a few little walks in the green of the countryside, with my gracefully aging maternal aunt. I bathed in the river—the municipal baths were disgraced by half-naked girls who presumably imagined they were on the overtolerant beaches of the Côte d'Azur. That sort of immodesty is an insult, a tacit mockery of all the female bathers whose bosoms are not perfect and whom aesthetic considerations, if not virtue, invite to modesty.

I was also curious enough to go through the archives at the town hall, and there I made some surprising discoveries about the former lords of the town, some of whom were brigands of the first order. You will observe that my curiosity now restricts itself to ashes grown completely cold.

My aunt arranged several times for me to meet a young teacher from Nevers who was there to take the waters with his invalid Mama and his basset hound, Candide. He is a very gentle, kind, attentive person. His conversation is interesting, educated, and sometimes funny. We met again by chance at mass, which is conducted very properly here and makes a nice change from the irritating whims and fancies in Paris. Louis wouldn't hurt a butterfly. We're very well suited to each other. He's writing a paper about the ins and outs of some of Voltaire's dirty tricks, in particular the disgraceful speculation that made Frederick drive him out of Prussia.

I'll come straight out with it and not beat about the bush: we plan to be married at Christmas.

I very much hope that things are sorting themselves out for you. When there are young children to think of, a separation—by whatever name—can only be a last resort, for which the main justification must be the moral protection of minors. And I didn't get the impression that the dissipation you once suffered from had become so public as to call for such measures.

I'll be frank: mightn't you yourself be partly to blame?

One evening you were kind enough to let me look through some passages of your notebooks which did not concern me, and I couldn't help being struck by the almost complete absence of the person to whom you united yourself for better or worse. The most serious thing, in my view, is not that you spoke ill of her. (It's your way to speak pretty ill of everyone, more out of pessimism than out of malice. Your critical intelligence makes you see only faults, and then exaggerate them.) No, the worst is that you spoke so little of the other half of yourself. Women can endure love or hate, but nothing drives them to undesirable extremities more than the depressing feeling that they don't count.

Think about it. And try to see more clearly what is there in front of your eyes. You may discover new charms, which if you go on neglecting them will be perceived by others. Have a little feeling for other people, including your too few friends, among whom I venture to count myself!

But true friendship involves giving good advice, and

not shrinking from disagreeable truths when they might be salutary. Please forgive me if I have vexed you; I have only your happiness at heart.

The two volumes are still being repaired, and will be there for some time. The expert who is working on them was involved in a car accident on his way back from his holidays. Fortunately his life is not in danger.

Take good care of yourself and yours!

I look forward to seeing you again soon.

Believe me, my dear Dominique, most sincerely yours.

Good simple prose! Good girl! May Louis the Well-beloved carry her away on the wings of dream, amid the dirty tricks of Voltaire! I have never been so glad my only charm is a critical intelligence, which is without a doubt what women like less than anything else in the world.

Once criticism leaves a woman's sex out, that shadowy opening, that well out of which Truth never comes, all that's left is an insipid sort of animal, and one who suspects as much. If you look in the encyclopedia, what do you find? apart from a few plagiarisms, what have women produced since they left the earthly paradise, and in particular since they became free to produce whatever they wanted? Children and female saints. But women don't want children any more, and saints are getting scarce. The female of the species is heading with much sound and fury towards well-deserved annihilation.

Good things come in pairs, and by the last post I received a very unexpected missive from Biquet-Lagravelle, dear old fellow.

Paris
Monday, the tenth of September, 1973

Alexandre-Ferdinand Biquet-Lagravelle
Member of the Académie des Inscriptions et Belles-
Lettres

Member of the Académie des Sciences Morales et
Politiques
Corresponding Member of the Académie des Beaux-
Arts.

Dear and honored Colleague:

I was not unduly surprised to learn that you were
the author of *Equivocations*. I had almost suspected
as much. Few people in the provinces, and not very
many in the capital, would have been capable of
such a feat, in which the virtues of the novelist are
matched by those of the linguist. The grammarian in
me is particularly touched by the latter.

There may have come to your attention an article
of mine in the *Revue of Comparative Grammar*, in
which I charged you—with the liveliest admiration!—
with five grammatical anachronisms, nine concerning
vocabulary, six concerning semantics, and six relating
to spelling. This in the context of an overall composition which is strictly and deliciously homogeneous: at
first reading it impressed one as a pastiche of the best
prose of the 1750s.

Certain errors do their author great honor, for while
a very few novelists have considerable insight into
grammar, grammarians like me usually make most
undistinguished novelists. One cannot possess every
kind of genius to the same degree, and I hope you
will not have taken it amiss that I valued the writer
in you even more highly than I did the specialist in
that very forbidding science which has been mine for
so long.

On the other hand, I was very surprised to receive a
note from your publisher, asking me to bring your excellent text to the greatest historical perfection I was
capable of (for it might well be that with advancing
age I could miss certain minor errors).

Monsieur Grouillot would, in fact, like to present
for the highly traditional Prix Fénelon, which this
year is being awarded on October 1, a novel similar
within a hairsbreadth to what one of the best authors

of the purest eighteenth century might have entrusted to the diligent attention of posterity. And there is still time to bring out a special edition in your name, differing from the first only in twenty-seven respectful corrections and a fawn sharkskin binding for the élite.

Such meticulousness does honor to French publishing, and probably cannot but affect a jury with which I have connections dating back to childhood.

But elementary delicacy makes it my duty to ask you for your permission. There are certain exceptional novelists whom an old man like myself could venture to correct only if armed with the author's most express and wholehearted encouragement.

Though it is not a pretty sight, I appear before you in all my nakedness: it would be very convenient for me if you could agree, for Monsieur Grouillot has been so flattering as to offer 27,000 francs to persuade me, and the roof of my manor house in Périgord needs repairing before the winter. But I imagine you too may be flattered to have your mistakes valued at a thousand francs apiece, and so perhaps be inclined to give me a speedy and favorable answer.

With best confraternal wishes . . .

P.S. There is a twenty-eighth (and gratuitous) error about which one may hesitate. On page 147 you write: "I hurried breathlessly up to the sedan chair in which my dear Clélie . . ." Marivaux or Prévost would have been more likely to write simply "chair." Who calls the subway the underground railway now? You probably meant to avoid confusing a modern reader, who might have been surprised to see a mere chair moving so fast.

This is far from being an unreasonable consideration. I continue to rack my brains. I should like to go into the matter with you.

Good, excellent, most excellent and delightful Biquet! Now, should there be a squall, we shall have nearly all the umbrellas in the Institut de France to shelter us! All that will be lacking is the barrenhearted scientists. But how could we work them into *Equivocations?* Their geometrical minds don't understand nuances.

Though my farfetched misadventure continues, my morale is better. It is as if the storms were blowing away with the coming of autumn, which already casts its vague mists over the river in the evening.

Cécile seems to be fixed up. Her restorer is still confined to his room. Saint Thérèse's orphans wax fat; the little socialists with as yet human faces swarm and romp in their splendid holiday camps. Thanks to Félix's tortuous intrigues, we're accumulating eminent protectors in case the worst comes to the worst, which is by no means certain, for temporary arrangements like this can after all be permanent enough to last for years. Fame smiles on me at last, without too much of a sneer. A jealous commentator might say the fame is that of another. But in a really social age isn't use better than ownership? I am what might perhaps be called the usufructuary.

The improvement extends even to my health, which seems to have been quite restored by six weeks in the country at my mill. And I've recovered my taste for certain merry games, which I intend to put to the benefit of the young architect's former mistress, who happens to be to hand. There's a good deal of truth in what the wise Cécile wrote, though I'd discovered it for myself before I got her reflections. I have a charming wife, whose lovemaking is sometimes rather moving: Claire is savoring her last soup before the dry bread of decrepitude, and it rouses her to feel she's sleeping with someone famous, whom she's long underestimated. A great author has just been born in her bed, and Madame is quite overcome.

A last favorable symptom is that the children reacted marvelously to the extraordinary news that I have some talent. Ever since September 4, the day of the revelation, Chantal has contemplated me wide-eyed and François has been very docile. True, in their presence I have been indulging in refined exercises in false modesty, and they are naïve enough to be impressed. To pass literarily from true modesty to false is to taste the food of the gods.

Of course, after he'd read *Equivocations* François lost no time in telling me, "You'll never get me to believe you wrote that! You must have pinched it from some attic!" But 51 percent of this perspicacious remark was meant in jest.

That lad will go far once he learns mistrust. Meanwhile, to keep him sweet, I've bought him a ruinously expensive Japanese motorcycle.

Claire has had to be content with a secondhand guinea pig cape. We mustn't forget that if she'd lived in Palestine under Tiberius I could have had her stoned to death and married some young girl. She's had a narrow escape! I'm going to remind her about it again in a minute before we pack up and go.

The strange thing is, it seems to me that since the success of *Equivocations* I resent more than I did before Claire's hasty deception. It's as if I were blaming her for not having foreseen the late blooming of a talent worthy of every kind of fidelity.

From the Diary of
Mademoiselle Cécile Dubois

9/29/73

It's impossible to see Dominique since he's been back in Paris! He's been seized and closeted away by Grouillot, who leads him a diabolical dance aimed at getting the Prix Fénelon, which he can put in for now that his pseudonym has been thrown to the winds. And not only is Dominique weak enough to let himself be maneuvered—though, alas, he has a certain amount of excuse—but the dishonorable extremity to which he's reduced doesn't appear to cause him any of the remorse it should. For all his complaints, I can discern over the telephone signs that he takes a dubious pleasure in being flattered and a sort of mischievous delight in helping to perpetrate a joke in bad taste. And terrible though it is to think of, he seems to have quite a good chance. It's not every day a Prévost is offered to that somewhat antiquated areopagus, and Grouillot is so lacking in conscience he's spreading malicious rumors about the other candidates. Lord, what a crew!

And friendship—not to put it any higher!—reduces me to silence. I must get into the habit of the basest complicity.

This morning, which is a Saturday, I had a new shock. In the window of a big bookshop in the boulevard Saint-Germain, I saw a beautiful de luxe edition of *Equivocations*, kid with gold letters, and plucking up the courage to have a look inside, I read with horror an exquisite preface by Biquet-Lagravelle apologizing for having made a few small corrections. Biquet-Lagravelle of the Institut, one of our finest grammarians, the paragon of disinterested learning!

And if Dominique is given the prize on October 1, I shall drink the cup to the dregs next day in Monsieur Grouillot's reception rooms, from 6 P.M. onwards. All Paris would be there to congratulate the winner, and I'd be there too, for once, because Dominique has invited me and I haven't refused. I almost want the impostor to triumph so that the reception can take place and give me the chance to see him again!

But to spend a fortnight without Dominique is becoming unbearable. I can't talk to him as freely as I'd wish from the concierge's loge—she's beginning to comment on how often I telephone. The few times of the day that I'm free, the post offices are closed. And the public phone booths are ruined by vandals.

But I have the right to see Dominique! In order to spare him any painful hope, and to shore up his marriage as far as possible, I've invented a fiancé (my first really big lie!). I've made the sacrifices that were incumbent on me. Our relationship no longer has anything suspect about it. I ought at least to have his presence, since I can't aspire to anything more!

And he issued the invitation so kindly I could tell he was missing me too. He took advantage of the first opportunity! And the good behavior I've forced him into gives him also the right to the comfort of a friendly presence. How alone my Dominique is in this hateful business, brought about by the most unforeseen chance! He needs my support, my advice, my affection . . .

How many dangers lie in wait for him! How many wicked

temptations may beset him! Especially as his time is his own—his lectures at the Sorbonne don't begin again until November.

When he told me yesterday, with a purr of satisfaction, that they were reprinting *Resurgences* in an edition of 7,000 copies, I could only express some friendly reservations. Was it really quite nice to profit from a reprinting that would never have happened without the intervention of the Abbé Prévost? Dominique said he'd think about it.

From the Private File of
Labattut-Largaud

Monday
October 1, 1973

At last I've emerged from prize hunting and all its platitudes. It's a real relief to get back to one's study and one's notebooks after all that frenzy.

Four hours' deliberation this morning! A record! Contrary to the hopes we'd been cherishing, it was a close and even epic fight: Félicien Bordescoule, the favorite among the other candidates, only just managed to clear himself in time of the accusations of plagiarism which Grouillot, with a sinister kind of humor, had spread somewhat prematurely about him.

After a tense period of waiting, I saw the door of the small drawing room in the Hotel Crillon open, a good hour late, and de la Pierre-Fondue appear, preceding his fellow members of the jury. A religious silence fell. Then the hoary orator put on his glasses, coughed, took a crumpled scrap of paper out of his pocket, and began to read it aloud.

"Ladies and gentlemen, I have the honor and pleasure of announcing that the Prix Fénelon has this year been awarded, by five votes to four, with three abstentions, to a work whose outstanding qualities will be evident to all. I refer to . . . er . . . er . . ."

Senility or sadism? Whatever it is, de la Pierre-Fondue apparently does this every year. One creates such suspense as one can.

"I refer of course to *Equivocations,* by . . . er . . . um . . ."

He wasn't able to finish for the uproar. The press, friends, admirers, those who were merely curious and up till now hadn't known which way to turn, flung themselves on me where I stood in the background.

Someone put a microphone into my hand, and when calm had been restored I spoke into it.

"To cut short overflattering compliments," I said, "I want, on this auspicious day, to make a painful confession: *Equivocations* is not mine . . ."

At that point I caught sight of Cécile a short distance away. I hadn't asked her to the morning rejoicings, thinking she wouldn't be free at the time the announcement was expected, and above all thinking the atmosphere wouldn't suit her. In any case, I was to see her at the usual reception the next day at Grouillot's, and enough is as good as a feast.

Cécile had assumed an expression of admiring and ecstatic terror, obviously inspired by her characteristic sublime naïveté: she was the only person present who took what I had said seriously. I gave her a very discreet wink to disabuse her, but she interpreted it wrongly, as a sign of complicity between martyrs trying to find a lion to eat them. And the jubilation on her face was all the more evident because the biggest lion was clearly destined for me.

I must admit I lost the thread of what I was going to say: my polished phrases fell into a black abyss, together, perhaps, with some vague sensations of remorse. It was a pity I hadn't provided myself with a piece of paper, like de la Pierre-Fondue, to emit two or three lines!

An uneasy murmur started to arise here and there, and I began to be filled with irrational panic, when the thought of Grouillot brought everything back to me, and I was able to go on, the sweat streaming down my back:

"As I was saying, *Equivocations* isn't mine. Indeed, it has been said that the plot is classical, that is to say of all time, and I am too ephemeral to lay claim to it. It has been recognized that the style belongs to an age when authors respected their readers and wrote quite naturally for future generations. So the style does not belong to me either. As for the spelling, that too belongs to the period! Only the mistakes are mine, and our friend Biquet-Lagravelle, who is here with us today, has lost no time in relieving me of them!"

(Knowing laughter from the audience; despair on the part of Cécile.)

I went on:

"In honoring this work the jury of the Prix Fénelon has endeavored to pay homage much more to a distinguished past than to that past's humble interpreter. It is first and foremost Mozart that we applaud in one of his symphonies, not the first violin, whose only task, together with that of many others, is to revive Mozart's memory. It is too often forgotten that it is the past that has made us what we are, until a more confused present destroys us.

"Such was the significance of the humble anonymity I adopted, and which I abandoned only at the pressing request of my publisher and of my many friends, and to which I long to return as soon as possible, convinced as I am that I have borrowed the greater part of my talents from writers to whom I owe everything.

"But personal anonymity would be no more than a hypocritical precaution if it were not accompanied by financial anonymity. And therefore the royalties of *Equivocations* are to go to an orphanage. A novel without a name will make it possible to give honorable names to foundlings, and perhaps to turn them into future readers who will never know the full extent of what they owe to our immortal eighteenth century.

"I shall end by . . ."

But the general emotion prevented me from finishing.

In the midst of all the crowd I embraced the highly impressed Chantal and François, and whispered to Claire, who had been shocked by the announcement of my generosity, "Don't you worry about the orphans! It's a put-up job with Grouillot—we're speculating on the side." And that wasn't far from the truth.

I managed to avoid Cécile, whose face was enough to take your appetite away, and was slipping away with the intention of lunching with the jury when a middle-aged lady bearing a certain resemblance to the Tower of Pisa fell on me and asked, "One thing in your speech intrigues me very much, Maestro. How do you propose to 'return as soon as possible' to 'anonymity'?"

I still don't know whether she was a fool or only pretending to be one. I seem to remember answering, at a venture, "It was a figure of speech, my dear lady. Rhetoric, as you no doubt learned at school, is the art of lying with the assistance of the most sophisticated of your audience."

It was a very decent lunch, and a rest from my previous sensations, whether agreeable or otherwise.

Despite the best of intentions on both sides, if this goes on I can see myself ending up by frankly hating Cécile for good and all. Fancy coming and standing there like the statue of the Commander at the beginning of my speech—confusing my mind, making me tongue-tied, and spoiling all my carefully calculated effects.

And what is this pest dreaming up for me for tomorrow evening?

I feel a kind of metaphysical terror, as if Heaven had appointed a guardian angel to signal to me every time circumstances led me into one of those third-rate actions that make up the major part of even the most honorable people's lives. As if Providence, through this ingénue, were every so often calling me to unusual perfection, and meanwhile trying to make me ashamed of myself.

I have to defend the most precious rights of man against Mlle Dubois: the right to moral mediocrity, which the new Catholic Church itself has been defending, ever since the Council, with the most farsighted energy. Perfection makes me tired! I'm getting old . . .

You end by chucking guardian angels like Cécile out of the window to see if they can fly straight!

My only consolation, and it's a meager one, is that my guardian angel feels only a platonic love for me. She phoned me again yesterday to lecture me, and took the opportunity to tell me to devote the cash from the new edition of *Resurgences* to the dogs' home. I nearly told her to go and jump in the lake. Who wrote the damned thing, I should like to know? The only decent thing I've ever written!

It's beyond bearing!

From the Diary of Mademoiselle Cécile Dubois

10/1/73

I shouldn't have taken the risk of going to the Prix Fénelon. I'm still overcome with sorrow and repugnance. Like a picture of hell painted by Breughel, full of people grimacing! What part did they make my poor Dominique play in all that? And how well he played it, as if he'd been expecting that vain and shameful mockery since he was in his cradle! How cleverly he managed the effects he produced, remaining silent and embarrassed after he'd revealed the deception, until a wave of uneasiness made even that blasé audience shudder!

I don't know whether I'll have the heart to go to Grouillot's reception tomorrow.

How am I to get Dominique out of this mess, this noxious atmosphere, and give him a chance to be himself again?

I didn't call him up this evening, and he must have been very disappointed. But I wouldn't have had the presence of mind either to congratulate him or to utter the reproaches he deserves. Moreover, it seems to me he avoided me at the Crillon. He couldn't have been all that proud of himself there under those Louis XV ceilings. Perhaps it wouldn't take much to put him back on the right path . . .

After Dominique disappeared I couldn't help going and offering a few words of comfort to Félicien Bordescoule, whose novel I found very pleasing. I told him how much I'd enjoyed

The Children of the Twilight and how sorry I was he hadn't got the prize . . .

But while I was uttering these banalities, which others were already echoing, I was filled with a feeling of shame and intense grief, which made tears come to my eyes and made me able to do no more than stutter and stammer.

Was it really right for me to talk like that, and could my sincerity in this case redeem my silence in another?

I was talking to a nice, talented young man who, with my tacit encouragement, had just been cheated of the thing he wanted most in all the world—a success that would probably have changed his whole life. I realized for the first time the extent of my responsibility!

I genuinely wept. Bordescoule, a sensitive southerner, was himself moved, and it wasn't long before a furtive tear trickled down his black beard. It certainly was the most painful and ridiculous misunderstanding.

"Oh, mademoiselle!" he cried ardently. "If only all my lady readers were like you!"

At that I fled.

I had the feeling I was imprisoned in an inextricable moral dilemma. But I soon realized this impression was false. In genuine ethics, ethics with a proper hierarchical system, there's never any real dilemma, because one duty is bound to prevail over another. Men start inventing dilemmas only when they're trying to find excuses for choosing whichever duty it is they prefer.

My own duty was clear, and I had suspected for a long time what it was.

When Dominique launched into his nasty little speech, I ought to have shouted out at the top of my voice, "To hell with the future of Grouillot and Company! To hell with Labattut-Largaud and his family! There's only one right involved here, and that's the right of Félicien Bordescoule to keep what belongs to him! *Equivocations* is a plagiarism of Prévost!"

But I was silent, and I know I'll go on being silent. I am capable of loving a man whom I no longer entirely respect.

I'm afraid God will punish me severely for it.

From the Private File of
Labattut-Largaud

Tuesday
October 2, 1973

Grouillot sent around the following note first thing this morning:

Dear Friend:

The news of your victory was conveyed to me by phone yesterday evening in London, just before I left for Paris. This development makes it more and more necessary that you should attend the twenty-fifth Book Fair in Frankfurt, which, as you know, opens shortly. Your laurels will arrive there in all their freshness, and this will greatly help the international sales I have in mind, and also make possible a useful publicity campaign.

I should therefore be obliged if you would, as a matter of urgency, at last come to a decision in the matter, and that in the sense most favorable to our interests.

The Park, the Frankfurterhof, the Intercontinental, and the Hessischerhof are already booked solid, but I could probably find you a room in a hotel that would still be worthy of your talents.

Try to give Edelberger a ring sometime this morning. Every hour counts.

Cordially yours . . .

My relations with Grouillot are improving, inasmuch as each of us makes a great effort to put up with the other whenever it's unavoidable that we should meet, whether publicly or privately. It's a marriage of convenience between a boa constrictor

137

and a gazelle he has difficulty in digesting. But for the most part the monster flees from the sound of my voice, and would rather dictate a note than have to talk on the phone.

I told Edelberger I agreed at ten-thirty. Not that going to the Fair at Frankfurt or anywhere else appeals to me any more than it did before. I'm allergic to mixing with crowds. What made me decide to go was the prospect of getting away from Cécile for a decent while.

Arrived at Grouillot's reception at about seven. It was a more brilliant affair than I'd imagined, with all the mob that usually frequents that kind of ceremony, and a magnificent buffet, a real set-piece it was almost a shame to disturb. Grouillot and Co. had really made an all-out effort there in the big reception room lit up as bright as day.

Cécile was there already, deep in conversation with some distinguished-looking young man who I prayed to Heaven was the pretender Louis de Nevers, come to take the waters of Voltaire at the Bibliothèque nationale. She was, moreover, wearing a very tight-fitting dress, which suggested love's awakening and for once did justice to her charms.

Betty Fitz-Delagrange fell on my neck, congratulated me feelingly, and told me she was sending me a case of Prince Consort brandy. Then I was got hold of by old Princess Babesco, of the Royal Academy of Belgium, who took advantage of the occasion to try to peddle her historic emeralds for the umpteenth time. The Princess is completely broke, and has got into the habit of selling her jewels for an annuity to one well-known person after another: no one tells them, to avoid causing anyone any distress. Some fight there's going to be at the funeral.

Anyhow, Grouillot had convinced the Princess to promote *Equivocations* in her Academy's bulletin. He doesn't overlook a thing. He's an artist in his own field!

Cécile then passed on to me her young man, to whom she'd just been lauding me and who therefore had a proposition to make.

"Frisquet from *Le Figaro*," he said. "We've just lost Lahure in the air crash in Guadeloupe. He was going to cover the Frankfurt Book Fair this year from October ninth on. We're in a jam. Since you're a German expert and have won the Prix Fénelon, would you oblige us by taking over from Lahure? You've only got to name your price."

Le Figaro pays well. We made a deal on the spot.

Frisquet was delighted.

"Splendid!" he said. "I'll send you the airline tickets and the hotel reservations."

"Why in the plural?"

"Oh, because Lahure always traveled with a secretary. Mightn't Madame Labattut-Largaud be tempted?"

I explained that Claire had to stay in Paris to look after the children going back to school.

Frisquet settled the matter with typical journalistic airiness.

"It's simplest not to change anything. If you don't use the other ticket it doesn't matter. Between ourselves, they're free tickets handed out by the airline for publicity. And if you don't need the second room in Frankfurt, someone else will be very pleased—you can't get into a hotel there for love or money."

I was very pleased to have the problem of where to stay solved so comfortably.

While Grouillot was chatting with Frisquet, I told Cécile that I had to go to Frankfurt anyway, but I was grateful to her for putting the job my way. She lapped it up. The girl has her good points.

With a sort of second sight she made much of the fact that a trip to Germany would do me good and perhaps free me of my "evil geniuses." Little did she know! The most irritating of the lot was within arm's reach!

What bothers me is going by air, even for nothing. I've got a phobia about flying. You can't see the country, and it's so unreliable.

I've been in three planes in my life. The first one forgot to put down its landing gear. Imagine trying to land with no legs. The second never succeeded in getting off the ground because it hadn't been properly checked. It didn't even attempt it. And the third landed at the wrong airport, the excuse being the fog. That was enough for me for a long time.

And these aerial peregrinations get more and more dangerous. Accommodating statistics calculate safety by the passenger kilometer. Why not by the passenger centimeter? What they ought to work out is the number of mishaps per passenger journey. If there's an accident every passenger light-year and I'm setting out on a journey that takes a light-year, I may as well be buried before I start. At least I'd save the money.

I was just meditating on my chances of arriving in Frankfurt all in one piece when Grouillot, who happened to be passing, whispered:

"Hang on tight to *Le Figaro!* They hate scandals, and are past masters at hushing them up." Damn that Félix!

I had the impression that just as she was saying good-bye Cécile was going to add something, but hesitated, waiting for something or other from me. Can she have some other practical joke up her sleeve?

Thursday
October 4, 1973

What a dope I was! The bombshell soon dropped, and what a bombshell! I was just having dinner and enjoying my onion purée when the telephone rang. Yesterday I had them say I was out. But I felt I ought to make an effort . . .

Cécile announced triumphantly that by giving up half of her Christmas holiday she'd got ten days' leave from the ninth to the eighteenth of October inclusive, which would enable her to make use of my second free ticket and my second free room at the expense of the paper. Her voice quite trembled at the thought of how pleased I was!

Caught like a rat in a trap. What excuse could I find that wouldn't sound offensive? In despair I tried hard to catch onto Gustave's tail, but that slut of a concierge has said she'll look after him.

No, there was nothing I could do. Impossible to say Claire might be jealous, given the state of our marital relations. Impossible to invoke the jealousy of Louis de Nevers, who is never mentioned now and never shows. Besides, our model friendship ruled out that sort of consideration. When Gustave gave way under me I had to welcome the pleasant surprise with all the delight of a gentleman of respectable age who'd be less lonely if he had an expert secretary with him. A librarian! What luck!

And I can't even say I'm not going. What reason could I give? I'm well, and I've practically nothing to do until November. Oh, why don't university professors have to do more work? It's not fair!

The more I think about it the more uneasy I feel. A pious fiancée doesn't pester a married man old enough to be her father, however sincere her friendship for him may be. There's a strong suspicion of something strange in all this. And the least touch of strangeness is dangerous. The novels of my fellow writers Boileau-Narcejac always begin with some strange detail, and the guy always ends up in the morgue before he knows where he is.

What the dickens does the girl want of me? Not love and not money. What then? It's enough to make you lose sleep.

Perhaps I'm speaking a bit too soon as regards money. It's true Cécile isn't venal, but there are plenty of different ways of being interested—or disinterested: it comes to the same thing once there are different ways of being it. It so happens that by chance Cécile knows a priceless secret. All around her she sees people making something out of *Equivocations* and doing everything they can to feather their nests. She may be saying to herself that it would only be natural if I tactfully made some gesture which would improve her own humble librarian's lot. Isn't that what a true friend would do in the circumstances?

In short, Cécile's persistence, even her sudden desire to take a vacation in Frankfurt, could signify no more than a gentle and implicit reproach.

If that's the case then there's a good chance that I'll be able to escape her assiduities once we get back from the Fair. While there's hope there's life!

I'm going to perform an experiment to clear the matter up. It's nearly 10 P.M. I'll send François—may as well make use of the Honda now that we've got it—to leave a polite note with Cécile's concierge, enclosing a check for 2,000 francs. We shall

141

see how she'll get out of that. The amount's a bit too large to be quite respectable. Subtle, that!

Anyhow, at last the young lady will have a good excuse for phoning!

From the Diary of
Mademoiselle Cécile Dubois

10/5/73

A charming note from Dominique:

> My dear Cécile:
> It's taken me two hours to realize! I can't accept the services of such a highly qualified secretary as yourself without making a proper payment for them. Please find enclosed a suitable check. It will enable you to do a little shopping and thus do credit to a "boss" whose "prestige" is rocketing (Should I qualify that with an exclamation mark or a question mark?). Please do accept it in the simple and friendly spirit in which it is offered. Forgive me for not having thought of it before, as soon as you called up with the unhoped-for news that you were going to come.
>
> Yours . . .

Such spontaneous delicacy suggests some moral scruples! How could I ever betray a man who writes to me from the bottom of his heart, and who thinks of me . . . as I think of him?

I must take my mind off all this by doing some work—bringing up to date the entries in the Petit Bonard that have to do with my subject. A million and a half copies a year! It's a handbook every student has on his desk—a regular gold mine! And the publisher gets students to patch it up every so often for next to nothing! I was doing it even before I had a degree! A nice vicious circle! But I shan't say anything. What's one case of collusion more or less now?

From the Private File of Labattut-Largaud

Monday
October 8, 1973

She didn't phone. She wrote.

> My dear Dominique:
>
> I am overwhelmed by your kindness and thoughtfulness. Of course I was thinking of staying in Frankfurt as quietly as in Bourbon-l'Archambault, and had no hopes of being able to see every day someone who has recently become so famous. I suspect you exaggerate a little the services I may be able to render you, as an excuse for being pleasant to me and letting me talk to you sometimes. But the suspicion is not so strong and certain that it can prevent me from trying to be useful to you, as you say you would like. You can trust me: I shall take my work very seriously and always be at your friendly disposal.
>
> Very sincerely,
Cécile
>
> P.S. I've looked up the most favorable union rates. Please find enclosed a money order for 1,500 francs. Thank you again.

She'll drive me around the bend! For the first time in my life I haven't the heart to write a single sentence. I'm flabbergasted.

Because of the confusion that always reigns at airports, where they're always losing both passengers and luggage, I thought to myself at three o'clock this afternoon that it would be more sensible to take Cécile her ticket. Then, if she missed my own departure for Frankfurt tomorrow morning, she'd have the wherewithal in her purse to take a later plane.

I arrived at her house at four o'clock. As the letter box was broken and the concierge, according to the note on her door, was "somewhere in the building," i.e. nowhere, I thought it safest to go up to the sixth floor and push the envelope under the studio door.

There was a gap under the door, and as I bent down I felt a slight draft on my hand. I think it was the draft that was responsible for everything. It suddenly reminded me that behind that door there was a mystery, while the occupant of the room was away, still working at the Library. And of course there came into my mind the temptation of examining that mystery more closely. After all the instances of Cécile's own curiosity, it would only count as a quite excusable indiscretion if I could find a letter from the aunt or the fiancé which would give me some inkling about the intentions of the person to whom it was written.

I was encouraged by the fact that the door didn't appear to be bolted, and the lock was cheap and flimsy. With the aid of my keys to the flat in the rue de la Pompe, it took me two minutes to effect an entrance. I bolted the door behind me.

I ferreted around for a bit. No trace of the fiancé. And the aunt's letters didn't mention me—only Gustave. She hoped he was quieter after the "outlets" he'd found in the garden during the Easter holidays. I was about to give up in despair when, inspired by the memory of Poe's *Purloined Letter*, I found Cécile's diary—lying wide open on the table!

I looked through it, then read and reread it for almost two hours, interrupted by the cat, and then by the voices in the next studio—a couple of illicit lovers who couldn't yet have had enough of it. Then I left the composition open at the page where I'd found it and fled furtively, a prey to contradictory thoughts and emotions, my mind completely confused.

How could I have been so blind? Such obstinacy recalls the famous saying, "They have eyes to see, and see not."

I must make myself be as calm as possible. No irrational fears, no panic!

At last I know all Cécile's thoughts. I know her better than a brother, better than a husband, better than a lover, better than a confessor, better than a concierge! So I'm in a position to draw up a strong, consistent policy and prevent anything irreparable from happening. It's really a most signal and providential piece of luck, my being able to get a look at that diary! If I'd had to go on struggling in the dark, I might soon have committed some fatal error. It makes my hair stand on end to think of it.

Now let's examine the facts quietly.

Cécile loves me. But it isn't the love she has for me that stops her from throwing me to the dogs, by means of a little note in the "concise" style Grouillot so admired. No, it's the love she imagines I return in my secret heart (as the result of, among other things, a fake novel, a fake proposal, and a fake caress)!

If she were in love with someone who remained indifferent, a girl like Cécile would end up yielding to the direst virtue, the sort that thinks of nothing but morals. The equivocations of *Equivocations*—and they are just beginning!—only make her grind her teeth. The one thing that reduces her to silence is the tenderness she feels at the thought that I love her. That and nothing else is my safeguard, my only safeguard!

In short, my reputation and honor, and those of Claire, François, Chantal, Félix, the Académie française, and so on and so forth, depend on my ability to play the ardent swain, an art in which I have never been very gifted.

So there it is. I've said all there is to say. Incredible but true.

The line I have to take is perfectly plain: I must sigh and yearn in as long-drawn-out a manner as possible in the hope that it will ward off the storm for a long time to come. It's a delicate situation, and as vexatious as it well could be—but not, on the face of it, desperate. With a devout, serious girl like

Cécile there's every chance that a strong feeling will last if it meets with the discreet response she looks for. Up till now I've been fortunate enough and innocent enough to appear to be in love without really meaning to, so it follows I should be able to produce the desired impression if I actually set about it. I may be blind sometimes, but I'm not stupid.

I think one might say there's nothing to get alarmed about in the immediate future. As for later . . .

God, what a bore! And I'm not out of the woods yet. When I say out of the woods, I should say off the tightrope—the tightrope on which I have to perform my antics with an alcove ever ajar on the one hand a yawning pit of lions on the other. Highly amusing!

I haven't told Claire that Cécile is going with me. What's the point of complicating matters?

I must finish packing . . .

Mustn't forget to take my current notebook, which is far from finished. The Park Hotel, where we're staying, is bound to have an even safer safe than the one here in the apartment. The wisdom of serpents must be the rule from now on.

How could a man as careful as I am get into such an unfathomable mess?

PART THREE

From the Private File of
Labattut-Largaud

Rather tiresome journey and arrival.

Before taking off kissed Claire, still half asleep. No waking Chantal. But François was wide awake, anxious for me to bring him back the latest Braun razor. To shave what, I'd like to know?

Found my secretary at Orly, gossiping with some junior officers of the press who were moving in two days in advance to prepare the ground for the general staff: the Book Fair opens on the eleventh. She was wearing a smart brown woolen dress with a coat to match, in which she might have been desirable to anybody else but me. I was extremely vexed to sense that those present took me to be a lucky fellow, but Cécile didn't notice the insinuation and I took good care not to bring the idea to her attention.

The umpteenth and most recent Middle East war provided a more general subject of conversation regarding conflicting and more or less repressed passions. When are Moses and the Pharaohs going to give us a bit of peace? Three thousand years is too long!

We had to hang about for four hours because of a wall of fog, and then came the police search and the hazardous flight itself. Cécile was in seventh heaven: it was the first time she'd ever flown, and she was flying with me. Three quarters of an hour later we were over Frankfurt. We had to circle interminably because the control tower staff was working by the rule.

Working by the rules, where safety is concerned, implies that in the ordinary way there isn't any security. When, because of a strike, some attention is paid to security for once, then there's a colossal traffic jam. Instead of having lunch we had to wait for a hypothetical permission to land, flying around for an hour and a half in an ever-increasing swarm of aircraft making sudden hops to avoid one another, brushing against one another with showers of sparks, sometimes crashing in flames into fields of potatoes, while the passengers, who'd been through far worse than this, went on reading their papers. I asked for the complaints book. Naturally, there wasn't one.

At four o'clock our taxi was driving past Frankfurt Central Station, an extravagant venture which the surrealist Rhinelanders regard as the finest building in the region. Three minutes later we'd arrived at the Park. Thanks to flying, I'd taken ten hours to travel some six hundred kilometers. A good cyclist could have done as much. It would have been quicker by train.

I didn't recognize the Park Hotel as it used to be. The old part had been done up, and an escalator, probably a spare part from the projected Frankfurt subway, led to a trio of elevators in a new building. But we hadn't got there yet.

The reception desk was expecting a Monsieur Lahure and a Mlle Takanoru. As Cécile couldn't possibly look less Japanese, the chief reception clerk balked. I was obliged to explain that as a flying coffin had liquidated the late-lamented Lahure in the West Indies, I had the honor of replacing him, together with the secretary of my choice. The clerk brought himself to sympathize, and handed me one key instead of the hoped-for two.

"You're fortunate enough to have a suite, sir," he said. "A sitting room, one bedroom on the right, another on the left, and they share a bathroom beyond."

This was a nasty blow. But hungry, thirsty, and dazed as I was, I still had the presence of mind to put on, for Cécile's benefit, a highly subtle expression combining delight at the unexpected proximity and concern for the reputation of a wandering virgin. I asked if we could have two ordinary rooms. They looked at me as if I were mad.

"But, sir, it's the Book Fair! Every room in town has been reserved for weeks."

Citing possible last-minute defections, I insisted on their

making a few phone calls. But it would have been rude to Cécile to make too much fuss. The fact of the matter was we were doomed to the Park and an alarming degree of intimacy, the legacy of Lahure and his proclivity for geisha girls.

With a trace of embarrassment, we moved in.

At five o'clock, after having sent down for a snack, I lay down for a siesta and succumbed to slumber.

I recall my dream beginning delightfully enough: I left the twentieth century for a well-deserved cloister, and Cécile took the veil, as in the film Bruckberger made from Bernanos' *Dialogue des Carmélites*. Then nightmare invaded the monastery in the shape of a horde of revolutionaries armed with pikes who drove Cécile into my arms. I was just crying out in the name of the rights of man when the ringing of the phone brought me back to Frankfurt: it was Cécile putting her secretarial talents to my disposal. I suggested politely that she should go for a stroll, and she took me at my word.

She didn't come back until nine o'clock, and then she was wearing a strange, preoccupied expression which I still don't really understand. I tried to distract her with my conversation during an excellent dinner in the larger of the hotel's two restaurants. But my efforts were more or less wasted.

One amusing detail was that the promenader's suffragette sensibility was offended by a notice she saw on several buildings saying, "Women not allowed."

"How is it possible, Dominique," she said, "in our day and age, in a model democracy, for a place still to be forbidden to women?"

"It means only girls are allowed," I said.

She wanted to know if they were convents.

I explained that they must be Eros Centers.

"Like mass-produced abortion," I said, "that's one of the most original achievements of humanitarian socialism or liberating democracy, which is based on the self-evident principle that a woman voter has the right to lease out the three instruments of labor that are her most intimate possession, provided the new morality is safe—i.e. unrestrained pleasure. The 'girls' live together like sisters; they are mistresses both of their own little rooms and of their revels, undisturbed by any unnecessary intermediary. You can't reproach the vice squad for keeping a paternal eye out for the modesty of any ladies who are behind the times and using posters to spare them the slightest risk of a misunderstanding that might bring a blush to their cheeks. 'Frauen Verboten' is simply honest segregation in a city which separates the sexes only in order to bring them together better.

"All that of course is theoretical. An Eros Center is really just a brothel, the same as in Barcelona or Buenos Aires—plus hypocrisy."

That gave Cécile something to think about.

She showed me one of the small ads in elegant italics on the back of the official tourist leaflet.

"Have a good time in Frankfurt! A charming companion is at your disposal in your hotel. Ring 442-442."

"It seems less hypocritical," said she, "but if possible, it's even more scandalous!"

I murmured, as a joke, "Why should I pay the earth for what's available free?"

Cécile looked upset. I'd have done better to keep quiet.

I'm sailing through dangerous reefs. I'm beginning to wonder if the atmosphere of Frankfurt really suits someone like Cécile.

My secretary having deserted me after dinner, I finished the evening in the bar, thinking about my liver to avoid thinking about anything worse.

From the Diary of
Mademoiselle Cécile Dubois

Frankfurt
10/9/73

Wonderful journey, Dominique charming—perhaps a little too charming. But I asked for it, so I mustn't complain!

It was the first day I ever spent alone with him, and the time simply flew. Less than an hour to leave the mists of Paris behind and see the roofs of Frankfurt appear between sweet little cotton wool clouds playing at hide-and-seek! What an advance on stagecoaches! I'm still quite dazed.

I've got a marvelous room, with radio and television and a telephone which links me automatically to the whole world. But I haven't anything to say to the world. I telephone only Dominique, who is no more than a few yards away as the crow flies! If it were spring and our windows were open this evening, I could almost hear him breathing, and writing in the notebook the things he dare not say to me seriously. How amusing to think I am doing the same, so close and unbeknown to him! We ought to write together, and then the tender harmony between us would be even more complete!

I am carefully storing up these unique and delicate memories, like a good housewife—why did they have to be polluted just by my going for a walk?

At the end of the afternoon, as Dominique had no need of my services, I went out for a breath of fresh air and to see what this unknown city was like. But it wasn't long before I didn't know where to look: it was like Sodom and Gomorrah rebuilt by the Marx Brothers! Everywhere there were shop windows full of extraordinary gadgets, enough to embarrass a monkey. And cinemas with indescribable posters and photographs, with close-ups of the wildest and most extravagant imaginings of vice. Bars and night clubs with entrances that flouted all modesty. Houses of debauchery, and outrageously indecent prostitutes in doorways. There were even television screens transmitting for the benefit of passers-by the lecherous dances and perverse postures of the cabaret shows. Then suddenly it was dark and the lights came on, crudely emphasizing the universal folly! I tried to escape and get back to a normal part of the city, but got lost in a labyrinth of streets and boulevards in which the same horror was repeated to infinity.

A young policeman with curly hair coming down past his shoulders—at first I took him for a transvestite—showed me the way back to the Park Hotel, which turned out to be quite close.

I asked the porter for an official map of Frankfurt, and got him to mark the hotel on it in pencil. He was a middle-aged man, and sympathetic. I hinted at my difficulties and said, "Is all of Frankfurt like that?"

He smiled, took up his pencil again, and suited the action to the words as he spoke.

"The places to avoid above all, mademoiselle," he said, "are the three boulevards that lead eastwards from the station—the Kaiserstrasse, the Münchnerstrasse, the Taunusstrasse, and the streets leading off them. For twenty years or so it's been a haunt of pleasure for the Fifth U. S. Army Corps and certain tourists from abroad and from the provinces. And the new regulations, which allow all sorts of license, certainly don't suit any respectable ladies who happen to be passing.

"But if you take the simple precaution of leaving the hotel from the south, towards the river, you go straight, so to speak —I once lived in Paris—from Pigalle to the Madeleine. On the whole, Frankfurt is a very clean city!"

I replied that from the little I knew of it, Pigalle was a temple of virtue and good taste compared with the Kaiserstrasse and its annexes. The porter shook his head sadly.

"Meet me in a few years' time in Pigalle, mademoiselle," he said. "I'm afraid the trend is irreversible."

Dominique, who's known Frankfurt for a long time, doesn't seem unduly bothered. Men consider the very lowest manifestations of sex quite natural. And I was hoping to lead him into a better moral climate! This is a fine start!

From the Private File of
Labattut-Largaud

Wednesday
October 10, 1973

I've just had a shock which suddenly brought back to me the precariousness of my pseudosentimental situation and is enough to give anyone the jitters . . . But I mustn't anticipate.

It seemed to me already yesterday evening that Cécile wasn't her usual self. The way she kept going off into her own thoughts, the way she found peculiar notices and suspicious ads, the way she ran away after dinner, as if she suddenly had something better to do than spend her time with me, or as if somehow my presence suddenly made her feel ashamed.

This morning she was still uneasy, and she also looked tired and had circles under her eyes. I offered to show her around Frankfurt, to take advantage of our last free day before the Fair began. She said she would rather take things easy, and at the time I didn't think anything of it.

So I went on my own and saw the reminders of Goethe, the Cathedral, the Römer, the old Jewish cemetery, and the Rothschild gardens. At about two in the afternoon, as the weather was fine, I went across the river and had lunch up on the Henninger Turm—the view was as splendid as ever. Then I paid a visit to the zoo: the innocence of the animals made a nice change from that of Cécile. At about six, going back to the hotel through dreadful traffic jams, I suddenly had the idea of stopping the taxi near the new theater, at the house of my old friend Julius Hallweg, the only interesting person I know in Frankfurt, really. The dear Herr Professor happened to be at home, with his spectacles, his wife, and his daughters, and they very kindly made me stay to dinner—the cold and frugal repast the Germans usually have when they dine by themselves at home. If the French hadn't invested first and foremost in their stomachs, they'd be the top industrial country in Europe. A delightful evening, enlivened by the elder daughter with some melancholy lieder at the piano. Enough said.

Shortly before midnight Julius came out with me as far as the street. It had got cooler, and he said, "There's a taxi rank not far from the theater, and if you're not lucky there, a long line of prostitutes with cars outside the Europa Hotel. They're very popular with rich Frankfurters whose cars have broken down because they don't mind taking short fares in exchange for a little conversation. The winner of the Prix Fénelon can afford such a luxury! It's the only improvement in the transport situation since you were here last!"

I chose to walk, as the Park was only a quarter of an hour away. Going up the Kaiserstrasse towards the station, I got the definite impression that the district's most noticeable industry had fallen off since my last visit, in April 1971. Not surprising in view of the depressing mediocrity of the goods offered. Street trading in sex is being replaced in Germany by private clubs of all kinds and door-to-door delivery by special truck. Eroticism is becoming interiorized, becoming something between friends and family, and no doubt the quality is all the better. Married women compete with professionals, and swap husbands like well-licked postage stamps.

At the soliciting entrance to a cabaret I just happened to be glancing at a full-length photograph of a girl more modest than the rest (she was wearing a minute black patch that seemed like a sort of mourning maidenhood heavy with obscure symbolism) when I had to dive under a porch to avoid a simply intolerable sight. There was my Cécile on the other side of the street, standing stupidly fascinated by the stills of the film *Exclusive Delights*. I was obliged to cool my heels there for five minutes before she and her shameful nocturnal curiosity moved on.

Yes, not an hour ago I saw it with my own eyes! Whose virtue *can* you trust in?

I realize now I must have underestimated the effect of the Frankfurt Sex Fair on such a simple and guileless soul. By the most unfortunate of chances it's particularly in evidence around our hotel. It's not the originality of the materials that attracts her. (She must have glimpsed some samples in Paris itself.) It's the obsessional ubiquity of this free light-and-shadow show, which is the same as in certain parts of Hamburg. It's a well-known fact that people lacking in experience are far more influenced by the pictures than by the words.

It's all highly bothersome and worrying! As if I hadn't got enough troubles!

It would seem that the unprecedented wave of pornography that covers liberal socialist Germany has a refrigerating effect on the sterner sex. Impotence is the fashion, and more or less genuine clinics are opening all over the place. The fact is that men are more virile when they feel that not to much is expected of their charms. They don't like to be overextended, either in the office or in the bedroom. To have to produce exceptional performances undermines them. They know that however hard they try they'll never come up to the hopes they imagine are being entertained of them.

Unfortunately women's resources are unlimited, as if a sympathetic Providence were trying to give them some revenge for the comparative passivity which is their lot.

As a result the German countryside is infested with maenads chasing after unfortunate satyrs cowering in the woods with their tails between their legs. The situation is even worse in the towns, and worse again in certain districts. And I'm in it up to the neck. It's in the Kaiserstrasse that the ratio of publicity to performance is most unfavorable for men and most flattering to women. I'm hounded by the most undeserved bad luck.

So I'll have to feel my way very carefully with Cécile. Don Juan, yes, but frozen by the first chill of autumn. Not a single frivolous word or meaningful look or equivocal gesture! It's impossible to tell which will get the upper hand with Cécile, pious disgust or satanic concupiscence. I'm sitting with an icy backside on a barrel of powder. The worst kind of powder. Face powder.

You would have thought a virtue like Cécile's would have been secure against a few pictures . . .

Fortunately the Book Fair starts in a few hours. That will give me a good excuse for taking my secretary in hand. I'll seize the opportunity to raise her mind to higher things, lecture her a bit if I get the chance. Even when the Fair itself is closed, I can dictate some short pieces for Le Figaro, general impressions and various items. That'll be better for the help than running after obscenities in the twilight.

An appeal to religion may also be useful. I've got plenty of trumps up my sleeve. She won't get the better of me!

From the Diary of
Mademoiselle Cécile Dubois

10/10/73

Got up late and spent the day resting, while Dominique renewed his acquaintance with this disconcerting city.

Watched television in my room: the Israelis don't seem to be doing so well this time. The Middle East problem has got so complicated you don't know where you are any more. When I told Dominique about my fears and perplexities yesterday evening at dinner, he just said airily, with his mouth full of fried scampi, "May the best man win!" That's the first reference I've heard him make to sport. But the days of the sporting wars our ancestors enjoyed are over.

This morning, before he went out, I saw Dominique putting his notebook in a compartment of the hotel safe. The bedside table is enough for me.

Sent a postcard of the choir of the Cathedral to my aunt. And another to Mlle Grivas, a view of the station, from the side, at dusk.

One wonders what is the real explanation of the abominations which disgrace the city right at the foot of that innocent edifice? The railway lines seem to bring travelers from every point of the compass to plunge into the bowels of hell.

Can it be the decline of religion? A revival of paganism among a people who were converted only late and superficially to Christianity? Reaction against a long period of official puritanism? An overzealous application of the free inquiry preached by the Reformation? But it would still need the right historical moment: a moment when a section of society is in league with a government that makes immodesty one of the rights of man. As if children too hadn't the right to be respected! I'm sorry to have to say it, but the municipality of Frankfurt could take lessons in decency from East Berlin!

As I can't move to another hotel, I must just adapt myself to and get the better of this shocking state of affairs. The early Christians lived in a world of debauchery, where, if you can go by *Quo Vadis*, Nero didn't hesitate to marry his minions publicly. That didn't prevent them from handing on to me something of their modest popular virtue.*

1 A.M.

I've just come back from a long walk in the streets near the hotel. The brisk night air did me good, and I'm beginning to get acclimatized to this dreadful display. The only way to appreciate the pointlessness of certain excesses is to study them closely.

From the Private File of Labattut-Largaud

Thursday
October 11, 1973

At ten o'clock this morning Cécile had circles around her eyes and was only half awake, as if she'd had a heavy night in the slums of Babylon. I inquired how she'd spent the evening, and she lost no time in giving an untrue account. A dangerous sign. My pupil is getting into bad ways. In the taxi, going to the exhibition center in the western suburbs of the city, I touched lightly on the subject of the Sex Fair, and slipped in a few home truths about its degrading banality and its lack of humor,

* Editor's note: Some grammatical ambiguity here. Does Mlle Dubois mean the pronoun to refer to the early Christians or the minions? Although the latter gave excellent examples of obedience and humility, it seems more probable that Mlle Dubois alluded to the former.

invention, and variety. The little hypocrite agreed with me, and the taxi driver stuck his oar in.

"It's just a booby trap for GIs and tourists from the South who've never seen anything. If you want the best you have to belong to a club, like the doctors and the lawyers, and that costs the earth. Porno's the same as caviar: you can have it if you've got the bread!"

Sour grapes! I shut him up by saying the refinements of vice were no better than the lowest commercial efforts. It's a good thing Cécile has neither the time nor the money to join a club! My virtue wouldn't stand much chance if she could!

Spent the day at the Fair, which can be described in a word: indigestion. Indigestion from the people—I can't stand crowds. Indigestion from the books, though I'd have expected I could get on better with those. But this twenty-fifth Book Fair consists of three huge buildings representing 3,600 publishers from sixty different countries—not to mention the forty-five special stands. Books up to the eyebrows. It's positively monstrous!

At least it's organized with the order and precision the Germans always exhibit when they put their minds to it. The French have never been able to equal it at Nice, where even the telephone is still at the planning stage. And a reliable phone service is essential at a gathering where a lot of national and international business is done.

One thing I find reassuring is that so far not only does *Equivocations* seem to be doing quite well, but it also looks as if it might get lost in the crowd and not catch up with me too soon. What is one book at Frankfurt? Or even anywhere else? At most no more than a shooting star.

Had lunch with Cécile in one of the six restaurants. She was still rather preoccupied. Met various organizers and publishing people, making use of the kind introductions Frisquet of *Le Figaro* gave me before I left. In particular, saw Edelberger at the Grouillot stand, in Halle 5, between the stands of Monaco and the U.S.S.R. *Equivocations* was in the place of honor.

Edelberger was very worked up and awaiting me eagerly. The big chief arrives tomorrow to conclude a big deal for the book, the culmination, according to him, of weeks of negotiation.

"Grouillot has refused so far, despite a lot of requests," he said, "to sell the translation rights. He thought time and the Book Fair would work in our favor. As soon as he gets to work here, he's going to offer the rights to the highest bidder in each of the countries in the running, dangling in front of them the advantages of a joint international edition, making use of the unique publicity supplied by the Fair. Several big fish are nibbling already and fighting each other to swallow the hook. It'll all happen in a flash . . ."

He couldn't tell me any more, as he was interrupted by a little Japanese minnow.

How I wish I could rejoice wholeheartedly at such news! But in this business one can't help wondering who is going to catch whom. However, there's nothing I can do to stop Grouillot. All I can do is hope he knows what he's doing.

At about five in the afternoon I slipped fifty pfennigs to the lady who looks after the washroom in Halle 5 before going to have a look at the German stands in Halle 6. In passing I said casually, "Fine exhibition, isn't it?"

She looked at me cynically.

"For all I can see of them from here, all fairs are alike to me. Books or hardware."

I damn near apologized. It's certainly true that ever since the thirteenth century the ladies in the washroom at the Frankfurt Fairs have seen a lot of water go under the bridge, most of it not very distinguished.

Cécile escaped me again to go ferreting around. I caught sight of her half an hour later among the two hundred German publishers in the hall opposite. At first I was relieved to see that she was with a nun, standing looking at the display screen of a venerable Augsburg firm, contemplating photographs used to illustrate a manual for the use of Christian families. But when I came up and looked more closely, over the nun's shoulder, I saw that the book was really some farfetched treatise on sexual instruction for children under the age of puberty. There they were, larking about naked, with their parents in a similar state of nature. I crept away on tiptoe so as not to disturb this primal innocence.

There's a certain fundamental naturism about the Teutons, an unashamed romanticism and naïve desire for do-goodism that delights in this sort of backward innovation. But Cécile is too old for it.

This was just another unpleasant incident. Ever since the girl got here she's undoubtedly been feeding on cheap obsessions. Whether it's in the Kaiserstrasse or with the modish Christian family, everywhere she finds material to inflame her imagination and excite her innards. It's bound to turn out badly if I don't take a hand.

When we got back to the Park for dinner I gave her a little lecture, without seeming to do so intentionally. As we were going to the restaurant we passed an aquarium in which one great big lobster was writhing desperately with his claws tied up. Cécile stopped to feel sorry for him. I explained that the tying of the claws was a highly ethical precaution, always taken in establishments of a certain standing. The idea was to make sure that before giving up the ghost in the boiling water the lobsters didn't indulge in some shameful pleasure in front of the customers and the young ladies who were their guests. But instead of laughing as someone with a clear conscience would have done, Cécile stupidly blushed.

To distract her from her imaginings I ordered a delicious dinner, rather as they used to stuff priests to stop them from going too often to places of ill fame. Ostend turbot with hollandaise sauce; saddle of venison with little chanterelles and charming scarcely nubile pears; distinguished Riesling and Traminer. The service of the Hungarian headwaiter and his Italian, Croatian, Turkish, and French assistants was beyond reproach. And I steered the conversation on to some points of moral theology that would have pleased the Cécile I used to know.

When we'd finished coffee I made her come up, rather reluctantly, to my room, where I dictated boringly for more than two hours: pages and pages, in the pure insipid style beloved of the unflappable *Figaro*, about the marvels of the twenty-fifth Book Fair.

What else and what more could I decently do?

Half an hour after midnight

Alerted by a nasty little nightmare, I just had a tyrannical whim and telephoned to my secretary to make a correction in what I'd dictated. All I got at the end of the line—such a short one!—was the silence of infinite space. The bird has flown again.

That really is something to worry about. To think I was afraid that if she came she'd be in the way!

I've never felt so lonely. I shall have an awful night, tormented by the apprehensions of a father and of a confessor, and with the additional anguish of Joseph in exile tangled up with Mrs Potiphar.

I shall be almost glad to see Grouillot. At least with him I know basically where I am, and I'm sure he won't hug me too tight.

From the Diary of Mademoiselle Cécile Dubois

10/11/73

I'm exhausted by a shattering day at the Fair. In a few hours I've seen almost as many books on display as there are on the shelves of the Bibliothèque nationale! The art books section was one of those of particular interest and richness. I can recall some Dürer reproductions and others from a fifteenth-century psalter that were exquisitely fresh . . .

Dominique seems perhaps less attentive, and the in some ways peculiar atmosphere of Frankfurt occasionally provokes him to moral reflections somewhat unexpected from the lips of a skeptic. I don't know what to think of such a strange reaction. What a difficult person he is to get to know, my "boss"!

I've just emerged from a lengthy ordeal which took place in Dominique's very untidy bedroom. He's certainly caught on to the *Figaro* style like a chameleon. It must be because he's used to plagiarism!

For a moment I was afraid Dominique might take advantage of giving me dictation to make declarations or too bold advances. But he behaved quite correctly, although the effort must have cost him more than he allowed to appear. I wonder what would have become of me otherwise!

I now realize how imprudent it was of me to come. But how was I to know I should be at his disposal like this, in a suite which makes all kinds of intimacy possible? I must pull myself together. It's high time.

The dictation has given me a headache. A little walk wouldn't do me any harm.

From the Private File of
Labattut-Largaud

Friday
October 12, 1973

At twenty past nine Edelberger phoned to let me know that Grouillot was at his stand, already in action, and that he'd be glad to have the advantage of my presence.

Impossible to wake Cécile: the night porter told me she came in at 2 A.M. I pushed a note under her door to say that I was calling in at the Book Fair, that I'd be back at the Park for lunch, that I was arranging for her to have a typewriter, and that I'd be glad if in the meanwhile she'd start typing out what I'd dictated yesterday evening.

Found Grouillot in terrific form, flitting about more energetically than ever, running from one stand to another for mysterious confabulations, and receiving important customers at his own stand.

He filled me in as soon as I arrived.

"Things are shaping up nicely. The English and Americans are interested. They think your book's deliciously French, discreetly sexy, slightly Freudian, but sufficiently restrained—a sort of *Love Story* written in clear, simple language that's easy to translate."

Then he gave me a dig in the ribs.

"You've surpassed yourself!"

Then he grew serious again.

"The Fair has rarely been so well patronized, and the prize and the film project will help drive the price up. Harper's, McGraw-Hill, Simon and Schuster, and Doubleday are still on the list for the U.S.A., and for England there's Hodder and Stoughton and Macdonald's. And once the book's taken in New York and London the other countries will soon follow suit. The really big deal is the U.S. But they're passing though a masochistic phase, and your book's unfortunately not anti-American. It doesn't spit on the flag or the dollar or the establishment. (It would be rather difficult for it to do so, seeing when it was written!) But I don't despair of working something out this morning with Simon and Schuster or Doubleday —they're not prejudiced. Anyway, thanks for coming. People like to see what they're buying, and you make a good impression—you look intelligent and honest."

Then he lowered his voice and took a piece of red ribbon out of his pocket and fixed it in my buttonhole.

"I noticed lately in Paris that you'd given up wearing your Legion of Honor, as if you were ashamed of having become as much of a scoundrel as a lot of the other people who've been awarded it. But wear it during the Fair to please me. It's good for another twenty dollars."

I couldn't very well give him a poke in the nose in front of the Doubleday representative, who had just come up.

I then had the privilege of listening to a very unconvincing conversation in English, in which Grouillot pretended to have an aversion for dollars and the American the same for any kind of literature. The gentleman from Doubleday had just half-heartedly improved his offer when Grouillot took a phone call from a literary agent in Hollywood who was plugging for him. He swiftly passed the phone to the visitor, as if to let him judge the news for himself.

The American hung up. He was visibly depressed; Grouillot was all sympathy.

"Mag Bodard has resold the rights to Metro," he told me. "They're planning a three-million-dollar picture. So of course we now have to discuss things with the U.S.A. on a different basis."

The idea of the Metro lion swallowing a plagiarism worth three million dollars, even devalued ones, gave me a hollow feeling in the pit of my stomach, and I didn't wait to hear any more. I wished them both good luck and went to stretch my legs at the next stand. It was the multifaceted Russian stand.

I found a secretary who spoke German with a Vladivostok accent and told her I was looking for a Soviet edition of *The Gulag Archipelago* from which to teach my children Russian. Instead of having a good laugh like any normal person, she put on a funereal face and said there was no demand for that kind of thing in the U.S.S.R.

"What about in the concentration camps?" I said. "You've got a captive audience of millions there. Another good coup you're going to leave to the Americans."

Having created a Siberian chill, I moved on. I shall never be able to keep up a long conversation with those people.

About half past twelve I went by the Grouillot stand again, and there were Edelberger and his boss looking like cats lapping up cream.

"Doubleday and Macdonald are in the bag," said Grouillot jubilantly. "And I'm due to sign in a minute with Fritz Molden for Germany and Austria and Rizzoli for Italy. [Let's hope Italy still exists when the book comes out abroad!] This evening I'll have got Holland with Sijthoff and Portugal with Europa-America. Only autumn, and it's snowballing already. Everyone wants to be in on it."

Edelberger having turned away for something, he added in a whisper:

"With the Metro movie deal on top of everything else, if there should happen to be an accident I'll bring out a special edition with a band on the wrapper saying, 'The plagiarism that deceived the whole world.' Then we'd make more money still, and we could cut off the supplies to charity."

He dinned a string of enormous sums of money into me, but I was only confused. In the position I'm in, what difference does it make—a lot more or a lot less?

I did say just one thing.

"I can see less and less relation between the basic product and the price. It's incredible!"

He laughed heartily.

"It's Frankfurt! You don't sell products here, as you naïvely put it. You don't sell books. You sell abstractions—desires, hopes, promises, reputations. And they take the form of rights, which produce credit, which makes it possible to make some money one day, with a bit of luck. You used to have a reasonable enough reputation. But I'm in the process of making you one such as you never had before, in order to sell it at a price you've never had before. It's only natural to sell what you make, even if it is only hot air. What would become of us otherwise?"

Had a late lunch with Cécile in the more intimate of the Park restaurants, and assisted at the termination of the lobster's sufferings.

Cécile looked worried and apologized for not having done the work. They'd brought her a typewriter with a German keyboard, which she had difficulty in using. So she'd gone to confession.

I had difficulty in concealing my relief. The secret statistics of the Vatican show that between 1895 and 1913 all the women who confessed to some mortal sin in the exhaustive catalogue concerning chastity waited an average of forty-eight hours and fifteen minutes before sinning again. It's nothing to laugh at. Forty-eight hours' peace can sometimes be very important to a man. The smallest moral progress has a greater calming effect than the building of a dam. Dams have never obstructed the course of vice.

"My own faith would, with God's help, have been the

stronger," I said, "if I myself had gone to confession even earlier. This very morning . . . I went to buy a razor for my son, François, in the Kaiserstrasse, between a sex shop and a cinema showing erotic films, and I, a man of age and experience, felt under attack again by the dismal obscenity of my surroundings. In such circumstances the eye tends to linger and the sin of complacence is committed before you know where you are, and in an area where a venial fault turns into a grave one as surely a bud turns into the soon-to-be-faded flower. When one goes through streets like that one should look only at the ground or up to heaven—though one would keep bumping into people, and how would you ever find a razor that way? The Archbishop of Frankfurt ought to set up field confessionals at each end of the Kaiserstrasse, in the hope that the guilty might be able to come to them without getting run over."

Cécile listened to this with all the compunction I could have wished.

After I'd digested the lobster I presided in person over the typing of my article on a more fitting typewriter, making more cuts than additions. A couple of articles should do the trick.

I rewarded Cécile with dinner in a typical old restaurant in the Sachsenhausen district south of the river, and twirled her around a few times in a waltz. Then I made her come to a performance of *Das Rheingold*. Wagner is boring enough to soothe the animal spirits, and you can usually count on the sure-fire comic effect of a heavyweight soprano smothering in her powerful bosom the squeak of a featherweight tenor. For once the circumference of the tenor was greater than that of the soprano, and despite all their efforts they never succeeded in actually getting together.

"The tetralogy illustrates the baneful influence of gold," I said to Cécile *mezza voce*. "But that didn't stop Wagner from chasing after money all his life. Here you see illustrated an even greater curse: the weight of the flesh, which makes sentiment ridiculous. Fortunately you and I make a more ethereal pair!"

I saw Cécile to bed myself, lingering in her room to the very limits of decency, and I watched over her closed door until the ray of light underneath disappeared. It took so long to do so I was afraid she might after all be getting ready to go out on another visual debauch. Availing myself of the rights of an enlightened tutor—and no doubt with the tacit approval of the deceased father—I risked a peep through the keyhole. You can see through easily into the bedrooms, but not through the main door.

In certain ways the scene I saw was reassuring: the young lady was in her nightdress, scribbling some lines in her journal. But her left hand was straying about and waving up and down between each sentence by way of punctuation, as if it were weighing out semicolons. Apparently confession is not what it used to be.

All things considered, I can breathe more easily. Prévost and Cécile seem to be letting up on me for a little while.

From the Diary of
Mademoiselle Cécile Dubois

10/12/73

An extremely agreeable day—setting aside the thorny and painful problem of the absurd absolution.

Dominique was quite charming again. I danced with him for the first time, and was hard put to it to hide my emotion. If he could have known what I was feeling!

Just come back from a magnificent performance of *Rheingold*, which I'd have enjoyed even more without the critical comments of my escort, who refused to shut his eyes to the physique of some of the performers. What does physique matter when the heart expresses itself in a clear and dazzling voice and with all the resources of talent? But Dominique is like that, and there's no changing him. I also have the impression that he's not so deeply sensitive to music as I am.

He lingered in my room just now with intentions that were

only too clear, despite various virtuous remarks as a matter of form. But it so happened that he withdrew before I ran the risk of weakening. Just a little longer . . . How precarious my position is! I can't go on forever giving him with one hand what I take back with the other. I've come to love him without too many illusions, but for that reason all the more sincerely perhaps. I really am to be pitied. How is it all going to end? I feel two Céciles within me which will never be able to agree. I'm torn, and it's all my fault. I can hardly write . . .

From the Private File of
Labattut-Largaud

Saturday
October 13, 1973

Disturbed again at an unearthly hour by Edelberger, who needed my presence for reasons of publicity. I thought it more humane to let Cécile sleep on after her efforts at correspondence.

Got through on the phone to Claire before leaving and gave her all the good news. Everything's fine at home: they're as proud of me as I'd like to be of myself when I have time to think about it.

At eleven Grouillot introduced me to the people from radio and television and the papers. First I was filmed together with the frightful Félix, who took up two thirds of the screen, then alone with my Legion of Honor. I replied with the least possible wit and good grace to a lot of stupid questions. Someone asked by what happy chance the idea for *Equivocations* came to me. I hesitated, and Grouillot answered for me.

"Familiarity with the classics!" he said.

There was a certain comforting truth about that in this sea of lies.

Emerging from the press (in every sense of the word), I was told by Grouillot:

"Sijthoff and Europa-America have signed. This morning I gave the Spanish rights to Plaza and Janes, who cover Argentina and Mexico. The Swedish rights went to Bonniers, a first-class firm, the Finnish rights to Weiling and Göös, and the Danish to Garfisk Forlag. For Japan, Hayakawa Shobo are trying to make up their minds. The Japanese pay seldom and not very much. But a Yugoslav firm, Mladinska Knjiga of Ljubljana, has had the curious idea of bringing you out in fifty thousand copies in Slovene, for a very interesting sum. State money, you see. They can afford these cultural gestures."

I spared a compassionate thought for the poor Slovenes, victims of the Frankfurt epidemic. But Grouillot hadn't finished.

"Tomorrow afternoon, Sunday, from six o'clock on, Grouillot's is giving a terrific reception in the big concert hall at the Intercontinental. I booked it more than a month ago, in the hope of being able to give your masterpiece a worthy international send-off—Gallimard and eight other publishers have just had a similar reception here for Joachim Fest's *Hitler*, which was bound to be a success. But there'll be eleven of us! And that's only a beginning! At the next Book Fair, I'll sell you to the Afghans and the Zulus and the Paraguayans, and to the Eskimos, who can't read or write—they can light bonfires with *Equivocations!*"

I left him to his lyricism and went to be photographed in daylight for various papers and weeklies. I posed in front of the hood of some exotic ambassador's Rolls-Royce—the funny little flag will probably be taken for mine. Then I chose for a background a dozen or so saffron-yellow Buddhists with sand-papered skulls, come to perform their shrill aubade on the flower beds separating Halle 5 from Halle 6. The row won't come out in the pictures. The people who see them will notice only the British elegance in the first lot and the mysterious spirituality in the second. That's the sort of detail that counts with the sort of public people like Grouillot feed on.

It was a good thing I hadn't brought Cécile: her scruples would have been awakened by the atmosphere. The Prix Fénelon only just scraped through. When I tell her what's going on I am extremely careful. I play down the business side and stress the precariousness of fame. I only hope it doesn't bring me bad luck!

But I shall have to invite her to Félix's reception, curse him. I'll tell her about it at the last minute, as if it's just a minor chore.

Edelberger tried to keep me till four for an interview, but I got away from him as soon as I could, after one.

Called for Cécile and took her to lunch in a Japanese restaurant near the Katharinenkirche. Some Neapolitan bellhop had told her about it, and she wanted to see what the food was like. She looked like someone who'd been seeing ghosts, which made me highly uneasy.

Between the dessert and the cheese—or rather between two viscous things, half flesh and half fish—she came out with it.

"Ever since I first heard of saunas I've wanted to see what they were like," she said.

My hair stood on end. Frankfurt is full of saunas of all kinds, but each one's more dubious than the last. They're a mixture of the hot baths of the Roman decadence, an aquatic brothel, and a massage parlor for sex maniacs.

Fortunately she soon reassured me.

"The porter recommended a sauna guaranteed by the town council to be respectable. And he didn't mislead me."

"The Frankfurt town council is a fine guarantee of morals," I couldn't help observing.

"For once they were irreproachable. When I went through the place, it was deserted. And when I got into the cabin, what did I find? Five men . . ."

"What!" I said in amazement. "You'd got yourself into a mixed sauna!"

"No one had told me. But that was only a detail. Although I deplore laxness on the beach I'm inclined to agree one can be more accommodating when it comes to collective hygiene. It's a question of habit and convention."

"If you like. But then what?"

"Oh, Dominique, it was horrible! There was hardly anything left of those five poor men. They all had arms or legs or something else missing. One had had part of his head blown off. Another was half blind. They seemed a bit surprised to see me there, and I was even more surprised to see them! But it would have hurt their feelings to go away. We soon got around to exchanging a few words. They were rough fellows, but nice. A man with only one arm explained that war invalids were admitted on Saturday morning for a quarter of the normal price."

All became clear. Cécile had happened upon a war veterans' reunion. The usual customers of the local sauna probably took care to keep out of their way, so as not to embarrass or be embarrassed by them.

"Do you realize," Cécile went on, "it was the first time I'd seen a man completely naked, and there they were all five in bits and pieces, and in a temperature of ninety-seven degrees! You can imagine how understandably upset I was and how this was followed by pity. Germany has obliterated almost all its war wounds, but those that can never be obliterated were suddenly there in front of me."

"If I know you," I said, "you were too considerate to cut the session short."

"Of course. How could I have acted otherwise?"

"And perhaps you said to yourself that these five heroes might have been deserted by their wives or mistresses. That their pensions weren't even enough to provide them with the melancholy compensations of venal love. That you had the most unusual and charitable opportunity, for a respectable maiden, of honorably offering people bereft of tenderness and carnal visions the most charming possible spectacle, made chaste, so to speak, by the surroundings."

Cécile looked down and sighed.

"My thoughts weren't as precise as that. But I admit I was taken aback by one thing that happened. The one who could scarcely see any more asked his friends to tell him what the intruder was like. And they, quite excusably examining me, took the liberty of describing me as pretty. Then the blind one asked me to hold his hand for a moment. 'It'll help me to imagine,' he said. Heavens, what a terrible thing war is!"

Tears were trembling on her lashes. I felt a gust of exasperation rising inside me.

"There's a fine thing!" I said. "As soon as I leave you for a moment, your wretched curiosity leads you into the streets of vice. And no sooner have you been to confession than you rush to perform a Christian strip tease for war veterans. You disappoint me. I wasn't used to such excesses in Paris."

Cécile placed her hand on mine.

"How hard you are, Dominique!" she said. "The way you scold me! What can I say? Except that what I went through today made me appreciate more than ever the happiness of having you near me and intact."

"Intact!" I snatched my hand away, not sure whether to laugh or cry.

"If I am all in one piece," I said, "it's because I'm careful. You wouldn't catch me scattering my arms and legs about from Stalingrad to Berlin and from El Alamein to Monte Cassino! And the fact that I still have the use of all my faculties is precisely what makes me warn you to be on your guard. I'm responsible for you, young woman! I have my faults as well as my virtues, but one of the latter is that I prefer hypocrisy to scandal, which ruins so many people every day. And anyway I'm one of the old school, and responsibility for a young woman is not just an empty phrase to me. It's very dangerous for women to put too much feeling too soon into matters of sex. From pious strip tease to the more frivolous variety is a swift and slippery step, believe me! Before you start wandering about, please ask my advice. That's what I'm here for, and I know the place better than you do."

Cécile, cooled off by what I'd said, promised to be sensible.

After the heat of the sauna she felt like getting a refreshing glimpse of the country. I hired a comfortable Mercedes, which took us among the lanes of the nearby Taunus mountains; they were less crowded than the main roads on a weekend afternoon. As the driver bucolically put it, "*die schöne Natur*" had cast the red robe of autumn over the thinning foliage, while the conifers were still the deep green of hopes that will not die.

It was a fine day, with a little warm, encouraging sun. We got out of the car to go for a short walk through the woods, among the mushrooms and the birds.

On the moss and among the bracken, couples of young

hominids were playing the beast with two backs. The females, who showed a marked superiority, waved their sterile white rabbits' behinds about, caressed by the sun filtering through the leaves; the males emitted plaintive cries. Sometimes one of them would try, in vain, to make a dash for it.

I made Cécile come back to the car. She was looking thoughtful.

As it was getting dark we found a peaceful country inn where we ate Schubert's wandering blue trout.

Cécile's eyes were blank and shining—it was the gentle languor of girls who want to do something foolish. The sauna had roused confused longings in her, and the mirages in the bushes had made them more precise.

I spoke with feeling, but to somewhat doubtful effect, about the curé d'Ars, that prince of confessors under the Second Empire, as we sat in front of a huge wood fire suggestive of hell, on which a woodcock was unavailingly roasting.

We got up and went.

Earlier in the afternoon the driver, a refugee from East Berlin, had told Cécile in a rather blurred voice the legend of the nearby Lorelei, mixing Brentano and Heine, nymphs and sirens, sirens and klaxons in a way that showed water was not his natural element. And he must have tanked up with beer in the kitchen while we were having dinner.

As we drove back through the dark to Wiesbaden and Frankfurt, he told us how he had escaped from East Berlin in the epic days, how he got across the wall of shame, how he just managed to escape the Vopos' bullets by running in zigzags. He summed it all up by saying:

"Brandt made the opening to the East. I made the opening to the West!"

This alcoholic Ulysses had a vocabulary like a rugby player or a hunter.

Zigzags had invaded his whole deportment since, and it seemed the socialists with wild beasts' faces still pursued him among the socialists of a ruddy countenance. Descending towards the motorway, we certainly performed more zigzags than the winding road required, and our wavering progress than continued along what was no more than an imaginary straight line, to which the person responsible tried to approximate. You might describe it as moral conduct.

Cécile took the opportunity to huddle against me with the energy of despair, as if such a dubious rapprochement could have put the car back on the straight path! I asked the driver firmly to keep as far as possible to a rectilinear trajectory. When we were still about twenty kilometers from Frankfurt, determined not to take cognizance of a bend, he dived into *"die schöne Natur"* like Baron Münchhausen's cannon ball.

When we opened our eyes again we found ourselves in a huge parking lot, brought up with no damage in the midst of a lot of other cars without any lights on. They were so many brothels there in the moonlight, shaking and shuddering with primitive life. The chill night air had made the hominids of the woods flee down to the plain, where the females had lost no time in shutting up the males in glass cages in order to finish devouring them.

Our driver, shocked by the enormity of his error, set off again at a funereal pace.

Cécile, also impressed by the strange circumstances of our escape, kneaded my arm and whispered, "But the Germans are always doing that everywhere!"

I reminded her that it was Saturday evening and we were among a nation of extremely hard workers whom two wars fought and lost and lifted to the heights of power and pleasure.

"My lectures ought to have taught you," I went on, "that ever since Tacitus the Germans have treated morals with the offhandedness, the *Gemütlichkeit*, the mixture of sentimentality and swinishness that was customary in the Garden of Eden, where they didn't know that they were naked. Eve couldn't tell the difference between Adam's sexual organs and an apple. The women of Frankfurt have rediscovered that primal purity. For me it has a certain charm—the purity of innocences lost forever. Latins can't feel comfortable unless they feel guilty. They're perfectly happy only when they're getting the better of their instincts. So take inspiration, my dear Cécile, from traditions which have proved their worth! In love not everyone can be a pig with impunity. You have to have the gift."

She was much struck by all this, and I was about to press my advantage when the driver suddenly emerged from the fumes of drunkenness to belch out a Lutheran proverb from lower Lusatia:

" 'A good pig is better than a bad priest!' "

The spell was broken. You can't say circumstances made things easy for me!

I prudently left Cécile outside her bedroom door.

Ten minutes later she called from the bathroom for me to show her how the shower worked—I'd already heard it working. She was wearing a toweling jacket, which fell open by its owner's desire. I withdrew without seeing anything. But she won't let me off a second time.

I was tempted to take advantage of her having a shower to read the rest of the diary. But what could the wretched contents teach me that I didn't know already? Depressed to a degree, I shut myself in my room and took the phone off the hook.

I know the day of reckoning is approaching, and I've exhausted all my defenses. It's as if all I'd done for nearly a year had combined to lead me into this trap here at Frankfurt, to be raped by a harmless virgin who wouldn't hurt a fly. It's a situation as humiliating as it is absurd. I shall fight to the end. It's a matter of dignity. But my morale's broken. I'm pessimistic. And tired of struggling.

And clear presentiments suggest what common sense alone would be enough to show: if by some misfortune Cécile, with the determination of a slug moving towards a lettuce leaf, achieves her goal, it will be the beginning of my downfall. To sleep with her would be no solution. It would upset an equilibrium which is my best, my only safeguard. With a mistress like that on my back, and her silence becoming more and more valuable, I'd have my work cut out to avoid dramas and even tragedies.

Why haven't I got enough faith to pray, and enough virtue for my prayers to be answered? The saints always wangle their way out. They only get themselves raped by men, which makes it less risky.

What terrible luck! My God, what terrible luck!

From the Diary of
Mademoiselle Cécile Dubois

10/13/73

I find it more and more difficult to resist Dominique. I have a feeling the day of reckoning is at hand, that I've exhausted my last defenses. Just now in the bathroom he'd only have had to . . . I dare not finish. His delicacy will have saved me one more time. But for how long?

And I see with shame that my weakness silences all the scruples the growing success of *Equivocations* really ought be making stronger every day, given the things I hear. O Prévost, O Bordescoule, how right you would be to despise me! You could never judge me more severely than I do myself! It's pitiful!

From the Private File of
Labattut-Largaud

Sunday
October 14, 1973

This morning I experienced something worse than sleeping with Cécile. Incredible!

My bladder was bothering me a bit about dawn, when I

woke out of a disagreeable dream, and when I came back into my bedroom I forgot to bolt the door again. How strange are the workings of chance! The most trivial detail can have the wildest consequences!

At half past nine, not being able to get me on the phone, Cécile knocked at my door. I was still half asleep and mumbled that I was coming.

If I'd had time to receive Cécile standing up, everything would have been different. But having taken my growl for an invitation, she'd entered the stronghold before I'd got a foot out of the bedclothes.

Dressed in a brand-new rayon dressing gown, she sat on the edge of the bed and spread typewritten pages out over my stomach. She had some criticisms of certain passages in my article. I settled the matter in a couple of sentences. She slowly gathered up her papers. There was a silence.

To confirm my usual tactics, a piece of good advice from Grouillot came back into my mind: "Mlle Dubois has to be managed by means of the Bible."

I had an inspiration.

"It's Sunday, Cécile," I said. "Where are you going to mass?"

And she answered wearily, "Oh . . . mass!"

I couldn't believe my ears. It was so staggering!

Reluctantly she explained.

"I go to mass to take communion, and I doubt if the absolution I received yesterday is valid."

My heart turned over. I begged her to tell me what she meant.

"I was shoved together with a group of people. A priest in ordinary clothes gave us a quick benediction. Then I was told I'd been absolved. Absolved without confession!"

"I seem to remember reading in Le Monde that Rome has authorized confession after absolution," I said. "What was to stop you confessing afterwards? Even if most connoisseurs don't."

"The Gospel."

"What do you mean?"

"I'm quite willing to receive absolution without previous

confession in case of shipwreck—that's always been done. But not in ordinary circumstances."

"Why, exactly, if you don't mind my asking?"

"Because the risen Christ said to His disciples and their successors, 'Whosesoever sins ye retain, they are retained.' How can a priest who hasn't got second sight forgive or retain sins he knows nothing about?"

I had no answer to that. I had the excuse that there wasn't any answer. Handling the Gospels is an extremely delicate matter. You need to start from the cradle.

I had another inspiration.

"If it's as you say, you must start again from scratch. Go and make an urgent confession to another priest, and he'll give you a perfectly valid absolution. And then everything's in order!"

She shook her head.

"I thought of that, of course. But if I don't tell the second priest about the first one's absolution I'll be deceiving him. And if I do tell him he'll say it *is* valid, so as not to go against his colleague."

We were in a dilemma of Byzantine futility. Since Cécile wouldn't remove her rear from my Sabbath couch either to go to mass or to go to confession, I tried desperately to think of another carrot to lure her towards the door. But my mind was a blank. It was like the oral in the agrégation, and being examined by Cohen-Gascogne.

"The difficulty's only temporary," Cécile went on more quietly. "When I've committed another really serious sin, I can add the sins I ought to have mentioned this time. But I'm not going to commit a mortal sin deliberately, just to be able to confess several. Don't you agree?"

The danger was getting closer. I was the most practical and handy mortal sin available for a swift general penance. Cold shivers ran down my spine.

I tried to convince Cécile that her absolution really was valid, but in my anxiety I improvised clumsily.

"Your problem turns on one word: 'retaining' sins. One verb out of four thousand pages of Scripture! You're being hypercritical. A social and progressive Church is not going to stick at one verb! Your absolution seems to me as satisfactory as it can be in a democratic age, when it's not a matter of changing men any more but of pleasing them. You must be wise and resign yourself to it. Let your priests absolve whatever they like, and God, Who is not mocked, will recognize His own!"

She suddenly burst into tears. Finally she came out with:

"You talk like someone without faith. But unfortunately you understand the facts. I no longer have confidence in the conciliar Church. I've shut my eyes like an ostrich up till now, but this business of confession is blindingly clear."

This unexpected reaction completely threw me. I tried to adjust with the rapidity of a computer. If Cécile had had enough of the conciliar Church, it would be disastrous to go on praising it. So then what?

I was dazzled by a third inspiration.

"I'm very touched by your trouble, my child," I ventured. "Your dearest childhood certainties have been undermined day after day for years by a lot of sorcerer's apprentices, with a contemptuous and doctrinaire disregard for your rights and sensibilities. But what have you to fear from a bishop or even a pope if your conscience is clear? That's what Luther said, and Paul the Sixth has been kind enough to rehabilitate him.

"Suppose confession does fall out of use? And absolution becomes, for you, rightly suspect? Suppose penance goes out of fashion and succumbs to the blows of Freud and unscrupulous theologians? What does it matter? Give up sinning and you won't need all that any more! I don't say give up sin—that's a vague abstract that covers a multitude of shameful transactions. I say give up all the actual sins that are yours and that you know and recognize, that the hours as they go by dangle before you. The sin of tomorrow, the sin of this evening, the sin of this morning perhaps. And if you still yield from time to time, confess to your guardian angel, who expects a lot of you, and who, I imagine, is sitting beside you in a white robe now, on this very bed."

I had laboriously reached the summit of my rhetorical, psychological, and theological abilities. The sweat was pouring off me. To do myself justice, no man ever defended his physical and moral integrity with more determination and intellectual agility!

The contagious warmth of my sermon and the sound of the beloved's voice had moved the naïve Cécile to the highest pitch of emotion. But she soon sobered up, and said with a lucidity that rather surprised me, coming from her:

"What a preacher you'd have made, Dominique! Why do those last wise sentences have to remind me of the model sermons the atheist Diderot drew up in the time of Louis XV for the Spanish colonies in the New World?"

I might have been quite annoyed. I observed with some bitterness that Diderot was doing it hypocritically, for cash, whereas all I had in view, setting aside all self-interest, was the happiness and honor of a troubled soul.

Cécile was again submerged in emotion, and the shame of having unwittingly wounded me redoubled the tears which before had gradually been drying up. A sudden impulse put her right hand on my left, and she couldn't help saying in an almost inaudible voice, her eyes lowered to the excessively low neckline of her dressing gown:

"I realize it is noble of you to talk to me about God, Dominique, especially as you don't really believe in Him, and it is against the most fervent interests of your heart. I envy you your strength! But oh, darling, it would be much easier for me to be perfect if you weren't there!"

There I was, nabbed again, and the smallest possible margin for maneuvering. It was worse than being with one's back to the wall: I had my back to the pillow.

I implored Providence to do something, and was lured by a fourth inspiration. I put my right hand affectionately on Cécile's right, which was clinging onto my left, and with an air of the utmost earnestness put down my last trump card.

"With your usual shrewdness," I said, "you've found me out. For a long time you've guessed what my feelings were. All you needed to do was to judge of their quality. Yes, my sweet darling, I'm not overburdened with piety! But isn't it my first duty, my first consideration, not to encourage you to do anything for which your conscience would reproach you sooner or later with a strength equal to your past virtues? Love might blind me for a moment. But friendship and respect doom me indeed to speak 'against the most fervent interests of [my] heart,' as you so prettily put it. I must take you as you are and as you have to be: impregnable! I realize my fate is that of Abelard after his accident, finding refuge and consolation in a spiritual friendship and in the fusion of souls at the highest level of exclusive delight. Let me sacrifice myself, then, and don't tempt me any more! My strength is exhausted."

Cécile's left hand made a great bound and came to rest on my right. To spare myself another long speech, I brushed my lips against the limp fingertips, which smelled of dubious absolution. This sentimental pyramid of hands surmounted by a crook's head drew from Cécile another cry.

"Oh, Dominique! You are too considerate! I haven't deserved to meet a man like you! Have I the right to accept such a cruel sacrifice much longer?"

There was no decent answer to that question. "No" would have been cavalier and blasphemous; "Yes" would have been boorish. It's by questions to which there are no answers, but for which they credit themselves with answers, that women trample over the most jealously guarded intimacy of their victims. They cultivate the flower beds of the implicit and grow roses that die and thorns that endure. The most stupid of women has a sixth sense which enables her to reduce the most intelligent of men to silence with disconcerting ease.

So I answered with a deep sigh, which Cécile took as sanction to fling herself sobbing on my bosom.

I was done. She hadn't given me a chance!

At half past eleven* I said at last to Cécile:

"It's the first time this has happened to me. But I'm not unduly surprised. History is full of examples of such failures in the first flush of a rare passion. Too much happiness jams up— very temporarily!—the works. When I came up to your flat to see how you were, did you not have a tender premonition and make me sit in a paralytic's chair?"

Despite my jesting manner, it eventually dawned on Cécile that I had to be alone, and she kindly withdrew.

* Editor's note: Rather than replace terms that are too crude with decent euphemisms, we have thought it even more respectable to make a large omission, which incidentally is in keeping with the incident concerned.

I collapsed, struggling against a nervous breakdown. There was indeed something worse than sleeping with Cécile, and that was making a mess of it.

I recovered my senses completely in less than an hour. The most important thing was to avoid overdramatizing. But it was urgently necessary to set the situation to rights. If I let the disease take hold, gnaw away at my innards by progressive methods, that "disease that spreads terror," the mysterious disease against which doctors, psychiatrists, psychoanalysts, and fortune-tellers all proudly claim the same helplessness—then I could expect the worst.

As I'd just told Cécile, there was nothing surprising about my having become temporarily impotent. After all the affronts she'd been subjecting me to for months, the final outrages were bound to finish me off. I should have foreseen it and prepared myself better for the inevitable. But was the trauma only mental? Had the severity of the shock and the feverish and hopeless trepidations not perhaps cracked some retort, disturbed some alembic, disconnected some syphon, blocked up some channel, coagulated certain peccant or peccaminous humors in the dark arcana of my physiology? Was I out of order only for Cécile, and to what degree? How was I to find out and get myself seen to in so little time?

Thinking it over, I realized I was just going around in circles. I tried to think about nothing for three minutes, but it was difficult. I glanced absentmindedly at the headlines of the *Abendpost*. The war was beginning to give off a strong odor of gasoline; you could smell it on the dead bodies. The page with classified ads was more amusing. The *Abendpost* is a big Frankfurt evening paper that's been going for twenty-five years and presents a special image of Germany in the dozen or so foreign countries in which it's sold. Every day a whole page is devoted to ads for telephonic prostitution. This, like the lonely hearts column, often contains pearls: "Adolescent tomcat from Siam ready to serve from 7 P.M. onwards"; "Lady translators, any language"; "Young masseur, Richard Burton type, will treat elderly gentlemen"; "Exciting Babsy (genuine black) will give you rose-colored dreams."

Nearly always the ad is headed "*Neu!*", meaning "new" or

"novice." A word that might once have meant virginity now marks the rapid turnover of mere livestock.

A little rose-colored dream wouldn't have done me any harm . . .

Why not pay a visit to Babsy? I'd never known a black woman. It would be a good opportunity to make a practical test of my machinery. The girl might be able to give me some expert advice, a trick of the trade, an old wives' remedy, a voodoo charm—at least it might work as a placebo. Professionals know much more about it than quacks.

The prospect cheered me up slightly and gave me the heart to go down and have lunch with Cécile. I ingurgitated an aphrodisiac meal, following the suggestions of the magazine *Er*: celery salad; pepper steak, rare; truffles "à la serviette"; and vanilla custard. A well-known publisher had just made away with the last rhinoceros horn in tartar sauce. Stupid things like that are good for the morale.

During the meal I made a praiseworthy effort and concentrated all my common sense and natural benevolence in an attempt to find Cécile reasonably attractive. We'd got to our present state through common faults, errors, and weaknesses. And bad luck had played the part it always plays when the cards are badly dealt. At dessert, with the help of a drop of champagne, I felt frankly sorry for someone with such an absurd fate. But good intentions were of no use to me yet . . .

Went up to Babsy's at four. Her commonplace studio, by an unfortunate coincidence, is in Sachsenhausen, near the restaurant where Cécile led me a dance two days before making an attempt on my modesty.

A pretty girl. Hair like a helmet of astrakhan. A slim vine that asks nothing better than to wind itself around you. Little tapered behind like a money box. Came back to life straightaway, but held back very strictly in hopes of more serious good fortune.

We mostly talked. Babsy used to be a teacher in Kingston, Jamaica. She's very hard-working and much sought after, and has given up seven years of her life with the object of saving up 300,000 DM and retiring, bottom light and head high. She's richer than I am already. I could do with some lessons in prostitution.

This intelligent and sensible young woman thought over my misfortune sympathetically and diagnosed too much cerebral activity. "You think too much, darling," she said. "Stop thinking, please, think about nothing at all, and it'll go like clockwork. I work with my head—it totals up marks and the rest of me doesn't feel anything. It's different with you—you ought to work with full trousers and an empty head."

I pointed out to her that to abstain from thinking when one was in the habit of it was no small matter.

"Well then," she said, laughing, "remember what they say in Kingston, and think about Princess Margaret!"

It wasn't the magic amulet, but the whole thing was worth thinking over. The consultation cost 200 DM. "Genuine black" comes as expensive as white.

Fairs and councils have always encouraged venal love, as Balzac reminds us in his *Contes drolatiques*, where the Belle Imperia "buttered up the cardinals" at the Council of Constance. And today in the *Abendpost* you can read: "The reading circle is at home from 3 P.M. to midnight. As Balzac said, 'The most beautiful woman is the woman of thirty.' Exciting! *NEU!*"

Such is the only constancy that can be counted on in this world!

Joined Cécile, who'd put on a short puce silk dress for the "Grouillot cocktail." I'd put on a dinner jacket. Cécile thought she should honor the gathering with her presence, but she had more urgent preoccupations than scruples about discretion. That was something, anyway!

The huge concert hall at the Intercontinental was overflowing with a mob whose motley clothes reflected the general mental confusion. There were sober suits, multicolored dinner jackets, lounge suits, "club" blazers and flannel trousers, sports suits. There were ties and open-neck shirts, hippy gear, Tyrolean costumes, and burnouses. And the women were wearing either ultraminute frocks or long gowns, miniskirts or gypsy petticoats, tailor-made suits, either severe or covered with flowers, bell-bottomed trousers or silk pajamas.

Grouillot came up to us looking like a hilarious Mao Tsetung, accompanied by a cowboy carrying a stuffed bird. He bowed to Cécile and told me how successful the party was.

"I think we've outdone the 'Bertelsmann cocktail' and the

Time-Life party both! And we're just as good as the Reader's Digest dinner or the Fratelli Fabbri cocktail, and they had the Fiat money behind them!"

I congratulated him, and left him to his cowboy, and we wound our sinuous way to the main buffet, where my presence gratified a few journalists.

We managed to get away from the mob scene at about eight.

As we came out, Cécile was shocked by a particularly long line of prostitutes in cars. She was beginning to get on my nerves.

"Ah yes," I said, "the world's a dreadful place, which pays no heed to the Judgment to come, and what you see here in the open you could see elsewhere behind closed shutters. We're the only two pure creatures in Frankfurt, my dear. Let's make the most of it!"

That shut her up till we got back to the hotel, where I screwed her with complete success.

Phew!

I must send Babsy some flowers.

From the Diary of
Mademoiselle Cécile Dubois

Monday
October 15, 1973

Since yesterday evening my happiness—delayed for a moment by a rather flattering whim of nature—has been complete. I rejoice! A joy so sublime and harmonious can't be very wrong. I can see the start of a great love that will harm no one. Thank you, God!*

* Editor's note: Great happiness, like the worst deceits, is silent. This mixture of stupid blindness and romantic blasphemy ends a diary which in places might have deserved a less deplorable dénouement.

From the Private File of
Labattut-Largaud

Monday
October 15, 1973

Last night I told myself that as far as Cécile was concerned I absolutely must get rid of my remaining reflexes of repulsion: the good will of the poor child is enough in itself to make such feelings quite unwarranted. And to acquire a minimum of inclination for that plump young body, which is as good as the next, the best thing was to make use of it as often as possible—at least at the beginning.

Woke her early. She was fast alseep, and looked quite touching.

As old Hugo says at the beginning of *La Légende des Siècles*:

> Précipité lèvres décloses plus ou moins,
> Des traces de vertu dans les plis du sourire,
> L'Ange déchu béat reposait sans témoins,
> Mais un soupçon de stupre aux babines du rire.*

I was tempted to behave badly. I sometimes felt I'd like to make the innocent creature pay for all the humiliation of my position, where my dominance only made me have to knuckle under more—punish her for all the harm she'd unwittingly done me. I felt like hitting, kicking, strangling . . .

But with the aid of education, reason, and self-respect I confined myself to giving the young lady a degree of pleasure she hadn't had the previous evening, the intensity of which surprised, even alarmed me.

From pleasure to remorse, from remorse to a confessor, the

* Translation: "Lips faintly parted, with traces of virtue in the folds of his smile, the fallen Angel who had hurried thither rested there blissfully unseen—but with a suggestion of debauchery on his grinning chops." Editor's note: This is of course another forgery.

descent may be swift. And any spiritual director worthy of the name would retain Cécile's sins until God was proud of her chastity and Prévost proud of her honesty. I should then lose both my concubine and my reputation. Probably the Council has patiently exterminated the race of confessors. But the genocide can't be perfect. A few old die-hards, persecuted and ridiculed, still watch out for the female penitent from behind the cobwebs of their worm-eaten kiosks, to remind her of the first rudiments of evangelical morals. If Cécile goes to the trouble of seeking, she'll find.

I must work at her *allegro moderato*. Little and often. More affection than extravagance. Mustn't ask her to do things that might prove too pleasurable. Must be calm and adroit.

We took a stroll around the Fair. This is the last full day. The book people pack up tomorrow and go at two in the afternoon.

Wanting to make a fuss over Cécile, I asked Edelberger for an advance.

"But I haven't got a penny here," he said.

"You're joking!"

"Absolutely not! In Frankfurt you deal in billions in every kind of currency, but only by signature or gentlemen's agreement—no actual money is involved. This is a fair, not a bank."

At this point Grouillot appeared and said kindly:

"I'll fix it for you. Grouillot and Company have got a whole lot of marks in Germany that they're in no hurry to take away —they're appreciating all the time. Would you like ten thousand to help you play the boy friend?"

As he was making out the check he said casually:

"Doubleday of New York, who've just bought you, give a private lunch party for about sixty people at the end of each Fair —for their international representatives and a few guests of honor. You're invited with anyone you care to bring—it's today at one o'clock in the reception rooms at the Park. I'd like you to put in an appearance, and as impressive a one as possible. Doubleday publishes about six hundred books a year, and publishing represents only a twelfth of their total activity. It's like a combination of Gallimard and Hachette that's been eating Popeye's spinach. You're expected to make a short speech. Very short. Outside the Senate, Americans can't bear to listen to more than three sentences at a time."

Cécile poked her nose in.

"I'd be interested to see that, Dominique."

So I was stuck with the speech.

As we were going off with the check, the odious Félix caught Cécile by the hand on the pretext of paying her a compliment.

"I am touched, mademoiselle," he said, "to see that you have had no scruples in sacrificing to Monsieur Labattut-Largaud all the virtues which once enabled you to condemn me irrevocably at Lapérouse. Dominique is a friend as honorable as I am myself, and in more need of being understood. Take good care of him! Grouillot and Company leave him in your hands."

Cécile turned away, very upset. I was torn between irritation and amusement.

"It's your own fault," I told her. "You forgot and called me 'Dominique,' and your happiness is written all over your face like an open book. You even seem to walk more gracefully. You must moderate your transports for the sake of your reputation —and that of my wife. You know, my darling, that I hand my own reputation over to you willingly. For what it's worth now."

Got my claws on the marks in a big bank in the Schiller-strasse, a quiet street in the old Stock Exchange district that's fortunately forbidden to traffic.

I'd never had so much cash on me at once. There were luxury shops everywhere. I bought Cécile a platinum watch to count the hours we were going to spend together; they'd seem shorter to her than to me. To the watch I added a gold necklace, which she made great difficulties about accepting.

I made an effort to persuade her.

"It's a sort of wedding ring—with the advantage that it's a collar and you could fix a leash to it. It ought to be me who wears it!"

She fidgeted up and down like a poodle.

"It's too much, Dominique!"

I produced another argument.

"Women in love are incapable by definition of being venal,

190

so they're free to act as if they were—conscience is on their side. You're not going to start disregarding your conscience now, are you? It would be the first time!"

The appeal to conscience won the day.

The jeweler was Jewish and, though Cécile didn't realize it, understood French. No doubt he was laughing up his sleeve.

You don't skimp on things if you want to keep a woman in style. I forked out another 3,500 DM to replenish a wardrobe that was in urgent need of it. If I have to have a mistress she may as well be properly dressed.

As we were getting ready for the Doubleday lunch and I was helping Cécile button up a new dress, I said, on impulse:

"You do love me, don't you? You've proved it unmistakably, by the most incontestable of proofs. But I'd like you to promise me something."

"What?"

"Never to betray me, whatever happens. Never to tell anyone what chance and your own curiosity led you to find out."

"But that goes without saying! If I kept quiet the day before yesterday, why should I talk now?"

"So I can sleep easily?"

"With both eyes shut!"

She kissed me on one eye, which was only semireassuring.

I asked her to swear on the Bible, but this offended her.

"I can't swear on the Bible to be an accomplice in crime just because I'm the mistress of a married man. Be serious, Dominique!"

I'd been clumsy. I asked for a less compromising oath, and she complied as follows:

"I swear to be discreet, by the very weaknesses I have for you, which will last my whole life long!"

Weakness wasn't much of a guarantee, and the suggestion of how long it was to last was a blow. But I had to force a warm and enthusiastic smile.

Then she added, with a gleam of mischief in her eye:

"Except in case of annulment, of course—as in marriage!"

I gave a painful start.

"Er . . . What do you mean by that?"

"I don't really know. But say I marry a charming young man, and on the morning of the wedding I notice that he's got a mole that he's kept hidden from me."

"Would you really call the whole thing off for that?"

"Oh, Dominique, love isn't based on the trust that follows union, but on the trust that goes before! If a man lies to a woman afterwards, it can be forgiven. But if he lies to her in order to win her over, it's moral rape—physical rape with deceit on top of it. A superfluous addition."

"But what could you have concealed from me, darling? The facts are so plain! And it's precisely what you haven't managed to conceal from me that's given you unnecessary gray hairs. So have the same unshakable confidence in me that I have in you. I need it so much!"

We embraced warmly. She'd managed to make me feel ashamed, which is difficult now.

As were waiting for the elevator to go down to the reception rooms on the first floor, a suspicion seemed to occur to her. She clutched me by the arm.

"You're not hiding anything from me, are you, Dominique?"

"But you've just said I'm not!" I naturally exclaimed. "You said yourself, 'The facts are so plain!' Darling, our story is history! The fall of the Bastille, told by Thucydides!"

"Facts can be colored."

"There's no need to color them when it's so easy to tell them straight."

"Swear to me on the Bible."

I started to laugh.

"Be serious, Cécile! Why ask me to do what you refused to do yourself?"

"I refused to call on the Bible in connection with fraud. But you can swear before God and man that your dealings with me have always been honest."

I felt a rush of panic. She'd cornered me once again with her primitive logic. But I wasn't going to be so stupid as to saddle myself with the Bible. One may be a skeptic, but skepticism itself counsels prudence.

But what intelligent answer could I give? I had to give it

straightaway. In a situation like that the slightest hesitation has the worst possible construction put on it.

The arrival of the elevator gave me a few seconds' respite.

As we were going down I managed, despite the dizzy feeling in my stomach, to say with a fair degree of nonchalance:

"On reflection, I think the Bible's a bit heavy for the simplicity of our love. And you can find anything you like in it, from the chastity of Saint Joseph to the concubines of Solomon and the weird goings-on in the Apocalypse. Let me swear before man—he was made in the image of God!"

She seemed satisfied. But what a narrow escape!

We sat straight down to lunch. Grouillot and Edelberger weren't there, and I didn't know any of the general staff or the international representatives from Doubleday. I felt like Banquo's ghost.

After the customary introduction I got rid of my speech.

"Mr President, Ladies and Gentlemen:

"I am extremely happy and flattered that the adventures of *Equivocations* are going to cross the Atlantic under the aegis of a great publisher who will, I'm sure, see that my wishes are respected and the book is given as unfaithful a translation as possible.

"Real translators have no scruples about improving what is entrusted to them, standing in for the author when he doesn't come up to scratch—it's well known that Shakespeare is to be found at his best in the language of Voltaire.

"So it will be in New York that the book finally attains all the perfection it deserves, cleansed of any lingering French accent, which is after all no better than my own accent in English.

"Bon appétit, gentlemen!"

I'd followed Grouillot's advice and reduced my speech to three sentences, each one shorter than the last so that the audience wouldn't get tired. My concision was applauded with enthusiastic relief.

Cécile, sitting on my left, observed, "A change from your lectures at the Sorbonne!"

193

An ambiguous remark.

"Did you find them too long?"

"No—I was looking at you!"

I glanced along the table, and thought I saw Monteilhet not far away. In profile he's got the jaws of a murderer and the nose of a vulture. From the front there's a disturbing hint of the sybaritic. The flat area at the back of the neck reflects his narrow-mindedness. From whatever angle you view him, you're never sure to find the same person—he manages to be like nobody else without being himself. What could he be up to with those hors-d'oeuvres?

But my attention was soon attracted by the neighbor on my right, a handsome dark fellow surrounded by pretty girls, all drinking in his words as from a sacred fount. I realized he must be another guest of honor, an Israeli, and perhaps a Jew.

I asked him politely for news of what was happening at the front: I'd rather lost sight of it, what with one thing and another. But he changed the subject.

During dessert I plucked up the courage to ask him again what he was doing at this gathering.

He then smiled, picked up my fork by the handle with his left hand, and started to stroke it with his right. The fork turned into a concertina before my very eyes. One prong stuck out sideways all on its own, but I couldn't make out whether that was intentional or accidental.

Doubting the evidence of my senses, I risked asking the young man to be kind enough to restore my fork to its original form, as I hadn't finished my cake.

"It would be too tiring for me," he said, "and the result would only be approximate."

To console me he lent me one of his forks, and told me his name was Uri Keller, or something of the sort, as if that revelation explained everything.

As I was rather listlessly finishing my cake, the vandal addressed himself to a big Britannica metal sugar bowl. He rubbed its belly like Aladdin rubbing his wonderful lamp, and the mouth of the sugar bowl twisted into a broad grimace.

I was as surprised as it.

"What sort of results do your talents produce with the girls, Mr Keller—or Geller?"

He laughed.

"The thing about girls is that they usually resume their normal shape automatically. I don't have to bother about it. Steel is another matter . . ."

I was surprised even steel could resist him.

"Have you a key on you?"

The key to the suite was at the porter's desk. The only key I had on me was the one to my safe. I hesitated for a moment. But there's a lot of difference between hotel knives and forks and a key to a safe made of special steel . . .

So without undue anxiety I put my precious key down on the tablecloth in front of Geller and watched.

The magician gently held down the flat rounded head of the key with his left forefinger and rubbed the narrow part of it with his right. Nothing happened.

"There's too much noise—I can't concentrate," said Geller, much put out. "Let's go outside."

"But talent is measured by difficulty," I objected. "You can rub it just as well here."

Stung, he girt up his faculties and gently stroked the recalcitrant tail to and fro. Before I could do anything, it bent upwards towards the sky.

A nice fix I was in now.

The rest of the company had followed these performances with the reserved interest of those who are afraid to appear naïve. They were presided over by the impassive John Sargent —he could afford a few knives and forks. But Cécile's eyes were popping out of her head, as if Jesus Christ had come again to feed the five thousand with three frankfurters.

I feared for her mental equilibrium, and decided I'd better get her away from this overwrought atmosphere for a moment. I slipped the twisted key into her hand and asked her to go down to the reception desk and ask them to supply me with a replacement as soon as possible.

When she came back a few minutes later and told me it would be ready at six o'clock, people were beginning to leave the table and gather around the celebrity of the day, who was now amusing himself with watches. By pawing their behinds he could make their hands whizz around.

"How do you explain all that?" Cécile asked me. Her curiosity had reached omega.

I shrugged my shoulders.

"It has to do with physics, and I'm no physicist. Perhaps some magnetic effect?"

She thought, and asked me another stumper.

"How could Geller, with the same magnetic field, bend knives and forks on the one hand and make watches do strange things without damaging the works?"

I was tired from my morning gymnastics and a little drunk on tokay, and all the more anxious to take an aspirin and have a siesta because the irrational disagrees with me. I suggested with a trace of impatience that Geller must have two magnetic fields at his disposal, one for forks and one for clocks and watches.† But more probably he possessed some glacial fluid which would pour out at the autopsy, and be bottled for the use of amateur conjurers and as an antitank weapon.

Soon after this I managed to get Cécile away from the evil doings, and suggesting she should buy some perfume, I said her time was her own until dinner. I adore perfume on women. Babsy smelled of sandalwood, virgin forest, escape. Escape!

Slept like a log, without any dreams that I can remember, until a quarter past six. No sign of Cécile. I hurried down and got my key—a key, anyway—and walked to the station, where I booked two first-class seats facing the engine for Thursday, the eighteenth. That would get us there on time. When you have the leisure and the means, you don't travel by air.

† Editor's note: That day Mr Uri Geller did not succeed in moving the hands of my watch, which, however, contained no steel: even the balance wheel was solid gold. But it did start to lose time afterwards. The maker's agent in Paris said it had been subjected to a strong magnetic discharge. After it had been through the demagnetizing box it was as accurate as ever.

But distinguished physicists have assured me that no known magnetic field is capable of distorting metal or affecting the works of a mechanism.

I give these details for what they are worth. They do not claim to clear up a mystery which remains inexplicable to competent and unprejudiced observers.

Cécile joined me in the hotel bar at eight-thirty, and we had a light dinner. I'd have liked to show her the Casino at Wiesbaden or Bad Homburg or Bad Nauheim. It's always amusing to see fools losing money. But Cécile felt a cold or something coming on and wanted to go to bed early.

So I went up to my room with my notebook under my arm and used the middle part of the evening to retrace in some detail the events of the day, as I'd already done with those of yesterday and the day before. I don't think I've ever lived through such decisive moments.

It's after midnight and I feel in great form. Pity.

Tuesday
October 16, 1973
7:30 A.M.

Last night at about one o'clock I really desired Cécile for the first time. I was encouraged by the light under her door. As she didn't answer the telephone I knocked, and eventually she answered that she was tired. She couldn't have been so tired she couldn't see me. The door was bolted. I made up some excuse and insisted. She must have thought that to refuse to let me in would make me suspicious, so she reluctantly did so.

I was surprised to find her dressed at that hour. And I was intrigued by a fresh inkstain on her forefinger. When you say you're exhausted you go to bed; you don't write your diary. Still less do you write letters. Without any real reason, I was seized by a sinister presentiment. I tore open the blotter and snatched up the following letter despite Cécile's attempts to get it away from me. At last she let me read it.

> My dear Dominique:
> I'm catching the 6:15 train to Paris first thing in the morning. I'm leaving behind all the things you gave me, except the watch, which will remind me of all the kindnesses for which I don't need to blush too much.

In the shop where I was buying perfume I met an elderly priest in a cassock buying incense for his little church in the suburbs. Despite the canonical rules he was good enough to give me urgent confession on a seat at the station. But the absolution is undoubtedly valid.

He of course insisted on sincere repentance, together with its fateful consequences. Within the hour I had sent a letter about the Abbé Prévost to the *Abendpost*. I have promised to bring our relationship to an end—but I haven't the courage to tell you face to face.

I hope your own conscience will enable you to appreciate the nature of my motives, and that the very honesty and depth of your feelings will soften the cruel sacrifice I impose on you in spite of myself.

I love you, and I leave you. I am grateful, and I cause you pain. I am more faithful to you than ever, and yet I betray you. What a dreadful affliction!

But in doing this I shall have helped to put the world to rights, as far as my humble abilities allow. God does not ask any more of His handmaidens. Though I forgot my own reputation for a moment, I could not bring myself to sacrifice those of Prévost or Bordescoule. To love one's neighbor is above all to act: no comment is necessary.

Your affectionate friend,
Cécile Dubois

I was stunned as by a clangor of bells, and didn't react at first. Cécile was silent, staring down at her slippers. I tried every kind of approach to plead my cause. Was it perhaps possible to retrieve the fatal note to the *Abendpost?* I must have wasted my breath for ten or fifteen minutes. I grew more and more anguished. Cécile was as cold as marble.

When I, quite naturally, referred to all the kindnesses which she herself mentioned in her farewell letter, those for which she didn't need to blush too much, but more particularly the others, she suddenly lost control of herself and looked at me with an expression that was enough to make anyone's blood run cold. The features I had always known as placid or loving were distorted with hatred, scorn, fury, and revenge.

The contrast between the letter I'd only just taken in and this access of madness was so sudden and striking that my anxiety gave way to a sort of confused panic.

"But what's happened to you?" I stammered. "What have I done to you then?"

This precipitated an outburst of downright hysteria. She leaped at my face with outspread claws, yelling coarse insults that could never have crossed her lips before.

"Swine! Crook! Filth! You dare ask what you've done to me?"

The railway confessor on his bench at the station had put the devil into her. How could her offenses against Prévost, cold in his grave these two hundred years, or against Bordescoule, whom she didn't even know, put her into this state? Even if you took into account her remorse for a brief roll in the hay. Ridiculous! As recently as yesterday she was so far away from the eighteenth century, so close to me and so grateful . . .

Recoiling in horror, I tried to make her be quiet. When she tried to bite me, I got hold of her by the neck. Her tongue stuck out and wagged about silently. In spite of everything I retained enough self-command not to want to stifle the insulter as well as the insults. As her eyes grew vague I loosened my hold. Her neck fell from my grasp. The body fell backwards. The side of the forehead hit the corner of the writing desk.

It took me some time to accept what had happened. Cécile was as dead as a doornail, snuffed out like a candle after mass or a banquet. I'd never believed that a fine healthy girl could die so fast, so easily, with so little effort. It was impossible to revive her.

In the end I lay the motionless object on the bed and covered it with a good thick blanket. I didn't really know what I was doing.

I swear it happened exactly like that. A dreadful, incomprehensible accident that was completely unforeseeable. There it is. And I'm not writing this to try to get out of it. What

199

have I got to lose now? Is this kind of murder like me? Do I look the sort of person who'd ill-treat girls and strangle them on moonless nights? I'm an absolute model of correctness!

It's nearly eight o'clock. For a long time I was prostrate, then I had a whole awful night in which to try to come to a sensible decision. But the factors of the problem are tragically simple, and they won't change.

Prison is what's in store for me. Appearances are too much against me. A prosecutor will have no difficulty in alleging murder for reasons of self-interest, murder of the most dishonorable kind, no difficulty at all in turning chance into an abject crime. And my notebook and Cécile's diary won't do anything to make the verdict any better—you can prove anything you like from them. In any case, I couldn't bear my notebook to be read while I'm still alive.

But I'd be glad if after my death the whole truth came out and both notebook and diary were read by impartial readers, who would judge me better than some chance judge or jury.

Chantal and François swung the balance and overcame my last hesitations. A father who committed suicide is a help in one's education. The stoical touch means you can hold up your head and discuss it with your friends. But what can you say about a father who's in prison and on hunger strike because he wants to be allowed to read *Le Figaro*? François and Chantal haven't deserved that disgrace.

I hope that one day they'll be able to read what I've written here and learn a lesson from it. Not to put the dead on trial, but to judge my life. It was really because I compromised that I got caught up in a concatenation of circumstances that could only end in disaster, this one or another. So there's a sort of logic about Cécile's stupid death. Do not compromise, my children! Never compromise about anything! If you start to cheat at marbles you'll find yourself fifty years later with a Watergate on your back, and all the hypocrites will point the finger of scorn at you.

I'm going to place these documents in a sealed envelope, with a covering note addressed to Monteilhet, who's roosting at the old Frankfurterhof. I'll ask him to do what he can to make them public; or to pass them on to François. Monteilhet has always got on my nerves with that limping copulation of sanctimoniousness and smuttiness out of which he tries to concoct a style, but true moralists are rare these days, and perhaps that old fossil may be the best one available to make his actions suit his words, and see it as his duty to ensure that what I leave behind me meets with a suitable fate.

Then I'll go down and ask the porter to see that the envelope is delivered. I'll come up again and telephone Grouillot and tell him I've strangled my mistress to help him with his publicity—thus bestowing on him one last pleasure.‡ Then I shall kill myself.

There's a Volkswagen in the parking lot under my window that's usually driven away just before nine. I shouldn't like to damage it as well as myself. I'll wait for it to go before I jump. Thus I shall die after due reflection, head first, and respecting the property of others. Perhaps that will be the final touch that will make my merits sufficient for me to enjoy eternity of happiness with my poor Cécile.

But my God, what on earth made her do it?

EDITOR'S NOTE:

When I first read the preceding documents I was struck, like Monsieur Labattut-Largaud himself, by the apparent inconsistency of Mlle Dubois's behavior. That is not to say that repentance has disappeared off the face of the earth, but people go about it in a different way. It progresses gradually through the meanderings of reason, the mists of the heart, and the convolutions of sex. It takes its time, so as to be more certain and more sure. It is never aggressive. In the case of devout girls who have erred, God is modest enough to veil His face and whisper His commands. He hides beneath the pillow and speaks in the night.

Cécile's conduct can have but one explanation, and that the most distressing.

‡ Editor's note: Monsieur Félix Grouillot, Chairman and Managing Director of Grouillot and Co., publishers, First School Leaving Certificate, Chevalier of the Order of Letters, member of the Wissam Alids, died of a stroke of apoplexy on Tuesday, October 16, 1973, at the Hessischerhof at three o'clock in the afternoon.

On the afternoon of October 18, having informed the Oberstleutnant in charge of the Frankfurtermordkommission, I went and questioned the clerk at the Park Hotel to whom, at about two-twenty on the fifteenth, Mlle Dubois had given the key maltreated by Uri Geller.

The clerk stated, "As a matter of urgency, the hotel can have a duplicate key made very quickly—provided it's during working hours. Any delay is in the delivery rather than the actual making. I told our guest's secretary that the key would be ready by six o'clock, probably earlier.

"When Mademoiselle Dubois came back from shopping just after four, the duplicate had just arrived, and I gave it to her. She seemed particularly glad about it, as she urgently needed to consult a certain blue file in which her employer had been keeping notes for some articles he was writing for a big French newspaper. She took the key and went to that little compartment you see over there.

"I was a bit doubtful for a moment. But the fact that Monsieur Labattut-Largaud had given her the key to his safe—even though it was broken—was a mark of confidence that gave me pause. Moreover, our guest and his young secretary were sharing the same suite and seemed rather—intimate. (I take the liberty of mentioning it because the papers already have!) I carried professional conscientiousness to the point of discreetly making sure that Mademoiselle Dubois didn't remove any money at the same time as the file. I didn't think it was for me to do any more. Put yourself in my place.

"Is this detail of any importance in this frightful scandal?"

I asked him at what time Mlle Dubois had put the file back in the safe, and he took me to see a colleague of his, who said:

"Mademoiselle Dubois put something in the safe just before six o'clock. Then she gave me back the key, as her employer was still taking his nap. I remember it quite clearly because Mademoiselle Dubois looked very unwell. She leaned on the counter for a moment and put her head in her hands. I asked if there was anything I could do, but she said there was nothing and that she'd soon be better. Seven hours later she was dead! Who'd have believed it?"

For working purposes I have had to read and reread Labattut-Largaud's effusions, that feeble union of rascality and beastliness, with the suddenly unsealed eyes of the unfortunate Cécile. I emerged from this testamentary ordeal greatly impressed. This must be the first time the public has had the chance to read so tame a piece of writing. Rereading it could only give pleasure to distinguished sadists or masochists.

Anyone with any altruism and accessible to noble pity must shrink from imagining the gentle Cécile amid the blue fumes of a Frankfurt beerhouse, among couples of satisfied lovers, herself searching feverishly for some words of love among the pages she had so furtively abstracted, but instead gradually discovering the staggering extent of her illusions. What a calvary between the first doubt, the first surprise, the first wound, and that ultimate cruelty: the sacrifice of her modesty and her dearest principles to a sneering phantom! And how crowding remorse must have strewn salt on the open wounds of her who had so recently become a woman!

The crowning shame was that Dominique had read her diary as she had just read his, and his artifices, which had begun by making light of friendship, eventually multiplied in proportion to the love she granted him!

Had any imprudent female ever been more deceived, and by a worse misunderstanding?

No, it's indescribable.

It became almost excusable for her to invent an act of confession to avoid giving herself away—though it meant she was soon to die without confession.

At all events, it is my fervent hope that *Death in Frankfurt* may enlighten the last surviving virgins about the infinite capacity for deceit of a certain type of graying seducer, and about the most deceitful type of all—the reluctant seducer! More selfish than the beast that unashamedly tears open its prey, he chases only his own wretched shadow through the labyrinths, shedding tears the while. And he lies worst of all when he's on all fours.

A family pet is better than an overfamiliar man, as Mlle Dubois once had the instinctive wisdom to realize.

In homage to her memory I adopted her dear little Gustave, who used to talk to me in the evenings about the studio in the rue Saint-Jacques and the paralytic Mama, and the vanished virtues of his mistress.

Alas, he has just been eaten alive by the Alsatian, and all that remains of him at the bottom of the garden, under the whispering palms, are a few poor hairs standing on end with fright and soon to be gone with the African wind.